BIGFOOT BOSS

CRYPTID BILLIONAIRES

LUNA CANTRIP

DEDICATION

*This book is for everyone who loves
flowers, cuddles, candy, wine, candles,
and also wants to get chased through
the woods and fucked into
the forest floor.*

CONTENT NOTES

Bigfoot Boss is an explicit monster romance. The book is a pretty light and easy read, but there are scenes of graphic sex, including some kinks that could be triggering to some. Please keep yourself safe, I want everyone to have an enjoyable reading experience.

Tags: *Instalove/Instalust, Fated-mates, Abandonment issues, Knotting means love, Money means love, If I throw enough money at this situation it will fix itself, You'd better run because you are really going to like it when you get caught*

CW: *Fat-shaming/Food Shaming (very mild and not done by the MMC), Parental abandonment (Discussion, it happening off page), Primal play, Strong language*

Mental health is important, if I missed anything that should have been included in the trigger warnings, please feel free to drop me an email:
lunacantrip@gmail.com

BOOK PLAYLIST

"BIG FOOT"...BIG BLOCK SINGSONG

"HAIR".. LADY GAGA

"RUN" .... VAMPIRE WEEKEND

"THE MOSS".. COSMO SHELDRAKE

"MEET ME IN THE WOODS"........................... LORD HURON

"IN THE WOODS SOMEWHERE"............................... HOZIER

"SWEET CREATURE"................................... HARRY STYLES

"MY HAIR"... ARIANA GRANDE

"MY BELOVED MONSTER"...................................THE EELS

"BIG ENERGY" .... LATTO

"BIG" .... TANK AND THE BANGAS, BIG FREEDIA

"RUNAWAY" .... AURORA

"LITTLE GIRL GONE" .... CHINCHILLA

TABLE OF CONTENTS

1

YOU'RE NOT MRS. MORTON

BAILEY

I don't think I 'get' abstract sculptures. Not that they aren't art, I just never understand what they mean. Take, for instance, the garden in front of my new workplace; it's filled with indiscernible concrete sculptures. Art should make you feel things, but all I feel is intimidated.

Maybe that's the point? Cryptech is one of those fancy tech companies whose office building is more like a compound. The temp company usually sends me places with beige cubicle walls, but this place has multiple modern buildings where all the walls seem to be windows. The lobby doesn't even have magazines for visitors to read, just a water feature and those see-through fiberglass chairs that collect smudges. My hands are too greasy to be around furniture that can show fingerprints.

"I'm here for the temp position. It's my first day." I tell the chic blonde behind the desk. She's pretty, with a starched white button-down and her hair pulled in such a tight updo that it makes me feel unkempt. "It's an assistant job. Mr. Kwatch. My name is Bay. Bailey Thorn, is the full name, but I go by Bay. I'm supposed to be assisting Mr. Kwatch." I fumble through my introduction, feeling, not for the first time, that the improv classes I took in college didn't actually prepare me to have real conversations.

Yes, and I should shut my mouth more often.

"You're working under Sacha?" The woman eyes me with pity. "He's gonna eat you alive. No offense," she adds quickly.

No offense was taken, until that last part. What the fuck was that supposed to mean? I'm not exactly in my element here, but in my yellow pencil skirt and pink blouse, I thought I looked more like a snack, not someone that could be devoured.

"Best of luck to you, but he's an actual monster. I wish I could give you pointers, but I've always avoided him. Thank you for calling Cryptech. How may I direct your call?" She switches to a phone greeting without even taking a breath and passes me a clipboard full of papers to fill out before gesturing to the empty lobby chairs.

I take the forms and wait until an HR lady finds me. She gives me a tour of the office. Everything in this building is either stark white or space gray. Even the people seem to be dressed monochromatic. I feel out of place in my second-hand blouse that I was so pleased to score for three dollars. I don't find a lot in thrift stores that fit a size 22, so I always snap them up.

I've been navigating the gig economy since I was seventeen. Working odd jobs for the past eight years, supporting myself through the fancy MBA program I thought would help land me a job.

Spoiler alert, it didn't.

I'm twenty-five, perpetually single, and struggling to find an employer who will hire me full time. Cryptech deals with some kind of tech that requires higher security; apparently, not many people pass the three background checks needed just to get through the door, so the temp agency sent the first person who qualified—me.

It takes half the day to check all the boxes on all the forms and acquire my temporary security badge. I'm passed from an HR person, to an office manager, back to HR. I'm introduced to more names than I will ever be able to remember. Until finally, after a quiet lunch of a PB&J and a granola bar that I dig out of the bottom of my purse, I'm sitting behind a desk with a pile of completed forms in front of me.

It's an assistant job. The desk's previous occupant apparently left for a better opportunity. Which makes sense, because almost every office worker I've met seems to agree that Sacha Kwatch is the worst.

"Nice to meet you, but no use getting to know our names. You won't last any longer than the others did," laughs the woman with long green hair who works at the desk across the aisle from me.

"Hush," the man in the cubicle next to her mutters. "You'll give the poor girl a complex. I'm Jacob, this is Tatiana. Kwatch might be a monster, but he's not going to fire you for no reason."

"He's had four different assistants in the last six months! I don't know what they're paying you," Tatiana crinkles her nose, "but I am sure it isn't enough."

They make their boss sound like an asshole, but they don't know how much I need this job. I'd work for the Jersey Devil himself for this hourly rate. The company must be desperate after the other assistants left because it's more than twice what I've been paid at any other temp job. If I land a full time job here, it would be enough to properly furnish my new apartment, pay off some of my student loans, and maybe even start saving for something bigger.

I'm settling behind my desk, when a voice calls from Mr. Kwatch's office.

"Mrs. Morton, the Iliad files."

I glance around, checking if there's someone else he could be speaking to.

A noise emanates from his office, something between a growl and a sigh. Did the CFO of this company just growl? "Mrs. Morton! I need you to update the Iliad files. Now."

I leap to my feet and hurry to the door. "Sorry, sir, were you talking to me?" I ask.

The office is large, and in contrast to the rest of the building that I've seen, this room is warm and moody. The walls are wood-paneled; opposite the door is a wall of windows, framed by dark, heavy curtains, neatly drawn back to let in the afternoon light. The middle of the room is a sitting area with a set of plush upholstered chairs. To my left, behind the desk, is a wall of wooden shelves, full of those kinds of post-modern-looking awards that rich people love giving each other. The desk itself is a dark wood, leather-topped desk, and sitting at that desk is a man. Presumably, Sacha Kwatch.

His head raises from his computer, catching my gaze for the first time. His eyes are large, dark brown, and soulful. He is also the hairiest man I have ever seen. His long red hair is slicked back from his sloped forehead and his even longer red beard is carefully combed in front of his tie. A sharply tailored navy blue three-piece suit complements his wide shoulders.

"You're not Mrs. Morton," he says.

"I'm not."

"Who are you?"

"Bailey. Thorn. You can call me Bay, if you like."

"Where's Mrs. Morton?"

"I think she moved to a different department, Mr. Kwatch. Sir." I swallow, trying to wet my dry throat. "I just started today. I'm your new assistant. Well, your temporary assistant technically, but I'm totally capable of handling whatever Mrs. Morton did for you. I'm sure—"

He dismisses my words with an easy wave of his large hand, and stands to a truly impressive height, eight feet at least. Probably. I've never been good at judging things like that, but this dude definitely has to duck going through standard-sized doors. Then, he steps around the desk and I see them.

His feet.

They are bare. His leathery toes dig directly into the dark gray carpet. More long red hair sticks out from beneath his pants. The feet are large. Big would be an understatement, but it feels like the appropriate moniker.

"Are you a Bigfoot?" I ask before I have a chance to stop the words from coming out of my mouth.

2

BE POLITE. BE CIVIL

SACHA

The unfamiliar woman's mouth makes a small, adorable 'o' shape, and her hand flies in front of her face as if to block the words that have already emerged.

"Is my species a problem?" I ask.

"Oh shit! Sorry, no! So sorry. Dammit, I didn't mean to curse," she blurts. "No. It's not a problem at all. I just didn't realize. I mean, it's pretty obvious that you are. A Bigfoot, I mean. I just didn't know before I came in here, so it kind of surprised me." Her mouth is twisted into a charmingly awkward smile now. "Sorry. It's not a problem. And I won't cuss anymore. Sir." She finishes the last sentence in a hurry.

"It's fine," I grumble, surprised that I actually mean it. I'm used to some of this behavior since the Decrypting. When technological advances and deforestation made hiding our existence more and more difficult, the urban legends started to reveal themselves to the humans, and cryptozoology became zoology. Not everyone has reacted well to our entrance into human society. Some people are shocked by my existence. Some even deny it to my face. I've spent half my life fighting tooth and nail for people to see me no different than a human and treat me as a serious businessman, not a monster.

However, Bailey genuinely seems more nervous to be talking to her new boss than she does about meeting a Bigfoot.

Her hair is dyed bright pink and styled in a short pixie cut that compliments her round face. She's wearing a yellow skirt and a pink blouse that highlight the impressive curves of her body, wide hips, thick thighs, and the roll of her stomach. I try not to notice how many curves my employees have, but she's like a vibrant flower in this desert of an office. I ignore the urge to dwell on that, though.

"Can you log in and update the Iliad account, Mrs. Thorn?"

"I'm—not sure, sir; I just started today. Like, I literally just sat down at my desk a couple of minutes ago. I don't know how to do anything yet. So I don't actually know if—" She wrings her hands.

I release an exasperated sigh. "Let me show you." I start to move past her, walking toward the office door. One step closer lets her scent hit my nose, and it nearly knocks me over.

Moss, mushrooms, and fresh rain; it's like the forest has invaded my office in the form of a shapely woman. She's perfect. She's meant to be mine. I need her. My whole body goes rigid.

"What are you wearing?" I ask, fighting the urge to hold my breath.

She glances down at her bright pink chest, broad and tempting. "Is it inappropriate? I've never worked in an office this nice before."

"The outfit is perfect—" I almost choke on my words, "—ly acceptable." I try to recover. "Are you wearing perfume or something scented?"

"No, sir. Just deodorant, I think. Is something wrong?"

"Nothing's wrong," I mutter.

Something is horribly wrong.

She's the one, the woman I am meant to be with, and she doesn't seem to know it. Another irritating aspect of humans. If she were a Bigfoot, she'd have known as soon as I did, but humans don't have fated-mates. My hand twitches with the desire to touch her; I clench it tightly into a fist. "Maybe you could switch to an unscented brand. The Bigfoot nose is very sensitive."

"Sorry, sir. I didn't know." Her nose scrunches.

But I know it isn't her perfume, it's all her that I am smelling, my mate. She's completely clueless about the bond.

I breathe through my mouth as I pass her, catching from the corner of my eye as she surreptitiously sniffs her underarm. I bite back a grin and step into the alcove that holds her desk. The space is bigger here, there's more air, and I can think a little easier. The deep desire to claim her fades a fraction.

"Can you log in, please? I'll show you how to make the changes that I need. You can do them yourself next time."

"Sure thing, Mr. Kwatch." She scoots into her desk chair but then pauses, looking up at me with bright blue eyes. "Actually, IT hasn't given me a login yet."

"Of course they haven't," I mutter. The universe seems to be trying to force my proximity to this woman. "Not your fault, Mrs. Thorn. May I?" I gesture toward her keyboard.

She nods, attempting to scoot out of my path, but in my hurry to reach the keyboard, my shoulder brushes against hers. The glancing heat sends a pulse straight to my cock.

It's a completely inappropriate reaction to my assistant. Humans don't operate on instant attraction like this; they don't take one sniff and know they are perfect for

each other. They take their annoying time with things like this. She isn't longing for me deep in her soul.

I have to put some distance between us, before I do something I'll regret. My fingers move quickly across the keyboard, pulling up her email and syncing her local folder with the network. I lean away and realize, in my haste to escape, I haven't explained anything.

She gives me a closed-lip smile, waiting for instructions. It's almost like the rest of the world goes fuzzy. She's meant to be mine; my prey. I want her to scream and run, so that I can catch her. I want to capture her soft thighs in my hands. I want to bury my face in her breasts. I want to taste the sweetness of her cu—

I shake the impulse from my head and take two steps back from her. I haven't spent the last fifteen years of my life trying to act human, only to be taken down by one single woman.

"My schedule is synced to your computer now. It outlines your responsibilities; there's a meeting at three in Conference Room C. Be ready to take notes."

She nods. I turn, hoping to remove myself from her presence as quickly as possible, but force myself to stop. Be polite. Be civil. Humans like you better when you act like one of them.

"Mrs. Thorn, I hope your first day goes well."

"Miss," she corrects me.

I raise an eyebrow in a question.

"I'm not married or anything. It's Ms. Thorn. Totally single." She laughs slightly awkwardly before biting her lower lip. I suppress the urge to bite it for her. "Or just Bay is fine too."

"Have a good day...Ms. Thorn."

I hustle to my office, reveling in a lungful of air that doesn't have her in it. My chest constricts slightly, my traitorous body wants to be breathing her in.

I try to get more distance from her desk, stepping to my wall of windows to focus on the view of the busy street below. My office overlooks Silicon Valley, the afternoon sun creating short shadows between the squat buildings. Countless hours were worked in this office over the past eight years. I was only twenty-two when my two closest friends, now business partners, and I built Cryptech from the ground up. It took sacrifice after sacrifice to make this business what it is today. I've spent so much time trying to fit in with the humans, until I became no more of a monster than any other businessman.

And now she walks in, and throws my world completely off its axis. I want her so badly that my whole body hurts.

But, hitting on my assistant? Awful.

Firing her on her first day so that I can ask her out? That definitely won't get me on her good side.

Stepping out of my office, demanding that she run from me so I can chase her down and mate her over the copy machine in front of the entire accounting department? Fucking her until she is screaming my name and so wet that my entire knot easily slips into her? Civilized humans don't do that. Monsters do that.

I have to take this slow. Give her a chance to warm up to me. Push down my monstrous desires, let her defenses fall, and let my prey come to me.

3

STINK LINES

BAILEY

Sacha is seriously intimidating, and seriously attractive. I can't remember the last time someone's voice rumbled straight to my clit like that, but he's already irritated by the way I smell. I guess the office gossips didn't lie about him being a jerk.

In an effort to avoid pissing him off any more, I sit nervously at my desk until the IT guy arrives. He's a skinny, bald man with glasses who shows me how to log into my computer.

"You're the new temp, right? Bailey?" His eyes travel up and down me appraisingly. "First days can be rough. How are you holding up?"

"Good. I think." I add the second part with a little laugh.

"Sacha can be a bit scary, but if you need anything, you can always message me." He gives a little wink. "I like your hair. Kinda makes you look like one of those anime chicks."

"Thanks. I think." I try to smile.

"Chris." He points to himself. "And it's definitely a compliment. I love anime." His grin widens. "Do you watch any?"

"I used to watch Sailor Moon every Saturday morning. Does that count?"

"Totally counts." He smirks. "As long as it wasn't Twilight or something silly like that."

"Oh, I kinda...like Twilight too..." I say, much quieter. No point in arguing with the IT guy when I need my computer fixed.

Fortunately, he doesn't seem to hear me as he repositions my monitor and launches into a long description of an anime I've never heard of before. Something that stars a pink-haired woman he likes. I don't follow much of what he's saying, instead leaning against the wall, trying to sneak a peek into my new boss's office.

I'm so curious about him.

His focus is intent on his computer, his large hands typing furiously. As far as bosses go, he doesn't seem that bad. I haven't really known any cryptids in my life. Since the Decrypting fifteen years ago, they've been slowly integrating into human society. I was only ten when it started, but I haven't run into many. A lot of them still avoid the larger more populated human cities.

So maybe all Bigfoots are gruff and stand-offish? Still, something about him is so intriguing to me.

His eyes lift, glancing toward the door. I jerk out of his line of sight, but we've already made eye contact long enough that I know that he knows that I was spying on him.

The guy is going to think I'm a creeper.

"I would not want to work with Mr. Kwatch every day," Chris mutters.

"Why's that?" I ask, my mind still half on the way Sacha's biceps pull at the fabric of his jacket.

"Why do you think? He's a monster. None of his other assistants could handle working under him." His lip curls in disgust.

"Working under him?" I ask. Is this a double entendre? Does he fuck his assistants? Is that why no one likes him?

"Yes!" Chris says emphatically. "He's a beast. Just because he owns the company, he thinks he can treat people however he wants."

"And no one's done anything?"

"What are they going to do? He's a genius CFO or something. They can't just fire him."

"I guess not." I shift on my feet. He didn't seem that bad, really.

"I'm sure you'll be fine though. Do you like sushi?" Chris surprises me with the new topic.

"Love it, actually," I say, grateful for the change of subject. "There's this great place, a couple of blocks from my apartment. West Side Nori. Have you been there?"

"I haven't. Maybe we could go sometime?" Chris asks.

"Go together?" I'm a bit taken aback. I don't normally date coworkers, but I could use any friendly face here at Cryptech. Chris isn't my usual type, but I guess he's kinda cute for a nerdy dude.

Sacha abruptly appears in his office door, his thick brows pulled together, a sharp glare aimed toward the IT guy.

"It's time for our meeting, Ms. Thorn."

"Right." I nod, grabbing a pen and notepad.

"I'll send you an email to set it up," Chris says.

"Sure, it's a date." I smile at him.

Sacha storms past, and I scurry to follow him to Conference Room C.

The conference room holds six people, other than me and Mr. Kwatch, I'm the only one wearing a color brighter than navy blue. Mr. Pleasant, the chief financial officer and a Mothman, looms above us from an enormous video conference projected onto one wall. His video is dim, highlighting his large red eyes, his feathery antennae wave around his head as he talks.

Sacha rolls his eyes almost every time the Mothman speaks, and honestly, Pleasant does seem like a bit of a blowhard. There's a lot of discussion I don't understand. Terms I don't recognize keep popping up: blockchains, hash codes, DNS. Things that I assume are computer jargon. I've never bothered to learn much about computer security, I was just super grateful when my browser started offering to save all my passwords for me. I threw out so many sticky notes.

It's a struggle to pay attention to the first forty minutes of the meeting, and as it drags into the second hour, with no end in sight, I begin studiously doodling in the margins of my notebook. When the Mothman finally logs off, I realize I've zoned out for the better part of an hour. When Sacha stands to leave, I take his movement as my cue to follow. I tuck my notebook under my arm and diligently trail my boss down the hallway.

"Can you type up those notes? Send them in a neat, bullet-point list. Do not use any of the fancy styling. I want to see it plain and simple. I need to be sure we have everything Pleasant agreed to in my records. We'll get you a tablet or laptop for note-taking in the future."

"Oh. Right. Notes. Yes. Right. I can type up my notes, sir." I walk double-time down the hall, trying to keep up with his long strides.

"You took notes like I asked, didn't you, Ms. Thorn?" His pace slows, so I can catch up.

I grin pathetically.

"I saw you writing the whole meeting, didn't I?" The corners of his mouth pull down.

"Not exactly writing, sir—" I clutch my notepad to my chest.

"What's on your paper, Ms. Thorn?"

"Nothing," I insist.

"It isn't the notes from the two hour meeting where I convinced our CTO we cannot afford the many upgrades he's insisting on? With the details of our lowered budget after negotiating for an hour?"

I shake my head, not wanting to answer.

Sacha scowls. The serious expression looks good on him. "Let me see."

He holds out one leathery hand and motions at my chest. My heart squeezes; I glance down at my notebook and back at him. Saying no now would probably be an automatic dismissal, and I don't want to get fired on my first day.

"Whatever you've written about me, I'm sure I've heard it before. I can imagine worse than anything you've said."

"Oh no! Sir! It's not about you!"

He raises one bushy eyebrow, a small movement that communicates that he doesn't believe a word I'm fucking saying.

"I promise! I would never!" I lean toward him. I'd hate for him to think I was writing mean things about him. Even if he is a grump who hits on his employees.

His empty hand is still outstretched. "Prove it."

I give him an awkward nod and hand over the notepad with a soul-crushing sigh. After years of rejection you start to notice the signs. This is about to be a classic Bailey Thorn, first day/last day job opportunity.

17

Sacha's hot fingers graze against mine as he takes the notebook. His fingers flex as he examines the page I handed him. There's a long moment of silence before he speaks.

"I see," he says slowly.

I put my full attention on the floor. I know I'll start crying if I'm looking at him when I get fired, and I'd rather not make a scene.

"Ms. Thorn," Sacha takes a deep breath, "is this a rather skillful drawing of our CTO, Mr. Pleasant, wearing a diaper and holding a rattle?"

"Yes." I sigh, pretending that there's anything interesting in the pattern of the gray carpet.

"Hmph." He makes the noise in the back of his throat, and when I finally glance at his face, there's almost a grin there. "And what are these?" He points to the swirls around the drawing.

"Stink lines," I admit.

A small scoff escapes his mouth.

"You've got talent, Ms. Thorn. That much is obvious." He nods seriously, still staring at the paper, letting the silence hang between us.

"I used to run classes at a paint and sip place, down on Market street. I took a couple of art classes in college. I was never super great, but I was good enough to run those kinds of groups. Mostly bachelorette parties and wine-mom birthdays, but it was a good gig! Until the store closed, the owner moved to Belize with her fiancé. Not that any of that matters now—" My explanation crumbles to a halt when his eyes dart up from the drawing to my face, and the muscle in the side of his jaw twitches.

"Next time, I am going to need you to take actual notes, Ms. Thorn."

"Of course, of course!" I insist. My stomach flips. I'm not in trouble at all?

"Just—send an email to Pleasant's assistant, Kara. Ask her to share her notes with you."

"Absolutely!" I breathe in a deep sigh of relief. "I mean, yes, sir."

There's another twitch in his jaw. I can't stop myself from grinning. I can't believe he isn't going to fire me. He's supposed to be a monster that no one can get along with, and here he is, laughing at my joke and letting me off the hook. I might be developing a little crush on him.

When I get back to my desk, I have an email from Chris in IT. He wants to set up a date for Saturday. I don't think he's going to be the one, but it's a nice distraction from the guy I'm more interested in.

4

RANDOM HIPSTER

SACHA

Magnes Loch strolls into my office without any preamble, ducking his long green neck to clear the door frame. The human-sized plesiosaur is wearing a dark gray suit—his usual color of choice—with an emerald button-down shirt under it. It compliments his scaly yellow-green skin.

The suit is a custom Brooks Brothers. I know because there's only one decent tailor in town who can make a suit for an odd body shape like one of ours, and both Ness and I use him.

Back in college—when Cryptech was just a start-up—Magnes, Pleasant and I could make do with t-shirts and whichever pair of pants we found in extra-tall, but these days, we have to look good to be taken seriously by humans. I don't mind the buttoned-up look, but Magnes really thrives in it. He was meant to be rich; he's so comfortable with the advantages that come with this life.

"New assistant? Again?" Magnes asks in his thick Scottish brogue. He still hasn't dropped the accent since he moved to America after the Decrypting.

I grunt a non-response from my sport behind my desk. "She's a temp. Just got here today."

"She's bonnie." The Scottish bastard twists his neck completely over his shoulder to peer through the door. I feel my blood pressure rise.

"Stay away from her, Ness," I say without thinking. For a talking dinosaur, he's always found it easy to sleep with humans. His accent, money and fashion sense seem capable of seducing any type of woman. He had a fated-mate once, but since Caddy left him, neither my heart nor my memory can keep up with the bevy of partners that sweep through his bedroom.

The dinosaur's head jerks back to me, and he raises one smooth eyebrow. The jerk has the gall to smirk. "Feeling possessive, are we?"

"No."

He folds his large frame into one of my chairs. He's technically a few inches taller than me, if you include his neck, but his limbs and torso are closer in scale to a human man. "You can be distracted after we close the Illiad deal."

"I'm not distracted," I reiterate.

"It's the biggest account we've ever had. It could double our capital." He continues the conversation as he pulls out his phone and uses his large green fingers to unlock the screen. Face recognition technology doesn't always work with his odd physiology.

"I'm the fucking CFO, I know what the stakes are."

"Double the capital means double the pussy." Ness grins lasciviously at his phone. "Until this is finished, I need you on your A-game, buddy."

"I'm fine," I snap. "I'm not you."

"Obviously." Ness snorts. "I know how to handle myself around women I want to fuck."

I hiss at him to be quiet. "I don't—" I stop, stepping past him and crossing to the door between my office and Bay's alcove. I reach for the handle and catch her eye; she gives me a gut-wrenching smile. Her blue eyes brighten, and her cheeks plump up as she grins.

I feel my face struggling to respond correctly. I hope she can't see the lust battling with sheer excitement in my brain. I barely know the woman, but my inner beast roars when she looks at me.

"You were saying, Sacha?" Ness laughs.

I close the door and whirl at my company co-owner.

"I don't want to fuck her," I hiss, hoping she won't hear past the door.

"It's okay if you do," Ness says before his face softens a little. "Just wait until this deal goes through. Then, you can go for it."

"You're ridiculous," I mutter, unwilling to admit my real feelings to him. I don't know how he would react if he knew I'd found my mate, not after his rejected him.

"I am," he grins, "and you have a thing for that woman."

"She works for me. The power imbalance is too high in my favor. It would be wrong. I—"

Magnes gives me a look of complete pity that stops me mid-rant. I realize I'm starting to sound like an obsessed fool. "Come out with me this weekend," he says. "There's a hot new cryptid bar. We'll meet some women who like their men tall, repressed, and hairy. You can find a random pink-haired hipster to take home with you and get your mind off of that one."

"I don't want some random hipster," I insist. I want her.

"Come out with me anyway! We'll get drinks, have a good time. You haven't let loose for a while, Sacha."

23

"No."

He leans forward, resting his hands on his knees, his long neck craning toward me. There's a moment of serious silence—something you rarely get with Ness.

"When was the last time you took a vacation?" Ness cocks his head to one side.

"What does it matter?" I ask.

"Pleasant and I wondered if you might want to take a break?"

"A break? Now?"

"Once we've wrapped up this case."

"I don't have time to take a break." I huff out a breath.

"You're stressed, Sacha."

"We're all stressed." I gesture between the two of us.

"You've been an even bigger jerk than usual. You need to take a break."

"We've all three been working nonstop since college to make this company what it is."

"You've been working nonstop. Pleasant and I have both taken a number of stops. He's wrapped around the finger of that terrible woman." Ness's phone pings and he glances down at it with a smirk. "And it looks like I've got a blonde pit-stop lined up for this weekend."

"I should finish the presentation this weekend," I grumble.

"You should go out into the world, get laid, take your mind off the pretty little lass."

I glare at him. She's mine. Nothing is going to take her off my mind. "I won't come into the office. Is that good enough for you?"

"What are you going to do instead?" he prods.

"I'll make plans."

"Staying home and thinking about your assistant while you tug on your little foot, isn't a plan."

"I'll figure something out," I snap. There are things I would like to be doing, with Bay, if she'd let me. "Sushi. I heard about a new place I'd like to try."

"Can I come with?" Ness asks.

I shake my head, "You wouldn't like it."

"How would you know?" He asks.

"Because they don't serve the sushi on top of a naked woman, Ness."

Ness laughs and smiles. "Fair enough. As long as you are getting out of the office."

"I will be." I ignore him. I'm certainly not going to tell Ness that I heard about the place while eavesdropping on my sexy new assistant's conversation. What he doesn't know won't hurt him.

5

NYMPHO OR SOMETHING

BAILEY

I'm only a couple of minutes late to my date at West Side Nori. Walking here from my apartment took a bit longer than I expected. I blame the red strappy heels, but tardiness is justified when you look this cute. They coordinate perfectly with my pink slip skirt and the red tank top. It was too good an outfit to pass up. I even have a pink jacket with little red hearts in case it rains. Which it looks like it might.

Chris is waiting at a table. His eyebrows go up when he sees me, and I hope that's approval, not irritation, in his smile.

"Hi, sorry I'm late." I slip into my seat, feeling just a little nervous.

"You are really dressed up," Chris says.

I blink a few times, trying to identify if that was a compliment. "I just like clothes, you know? Fashion is such a fun way to express yourself. I worked in a vintage shop for a couple of months in college and there were so many great finds. I had to quit because I usually spent most of my paycheck before I got it—" I trail off realizing that he's wearing a pair of faded-blue jeans and

27

a threadbare t-shirt that probably fit him a few years ago. "Of course, everyone should wear whatever they're comfortable in."

"Of course." His mouth turns up in smile that isn't quite nice.

"How do you feel about a Philadelphia roll? I'm absolutely starving."

"I'm sure you are."

The comment catches me sideways. "I didn't eat much for lunch," I shift in my seat, "so I'll probably get the seaweed salad as well, and maybe a spicy tuna roll. What are you thinking? Do you want to split something?"

Chris laughs, and this one definitely doesn't feel nice. He lists off something that's a bit too raw for my taste before leaning forward to ask, "Can I ask you about that girl with the green hair?"

"Tatiana?" I clarify. The woman who works across the aisle from me. She's pretty, with long hair in small braids that hang down to her waist.

"Yeah, what's her deal? Is she a nympho or something?"

"Do you mean like a water nymph?" I think that's one of the monsters that joined society after the Decrypting.

"It's the same thing, isn't it?" He smirks.

"No. I really don't think it is." His words turn my stomach a little. "I think she's just a human with green hair. She's nice for the most part, I think."

"So, you do know her?" He continues his thought before I even have a chance to respond, "Do you know if she's single or anything?"

"Wh—What?"

"Tatiana. Do you think she'd go out with me? Or does she have a boyfriend?"

"That feels inappropriate to ask."

"Why? Is she a lesbian?"

"Do you always ask about other women while you are on a date?"

"Date?" His face contorts into a smile that definitely isn't nice. "Oh, did you think this was a date?"

"I did think that. I guess I misunderstood."

"No! No way!" He's far too enthusiastic with that response.

"It's alright. I guess I got my wires crossed."

"I mean—I wouldn't date a girl like you." He grimaces. "Not that you aren't pretty. You have a nice face. You could probably be a model, you know, if you lost like fifty or seventy pounds. Something like that?"

"Alright," I say, standing from the table so suddenly the soy sauce bottles jingle. "I think that's enough for the night."

"What? You can't even have dinner with me now?"

I shake my head. "I'm not going to let this terrible non-date go on any longer. I like this restaurant. I want to come back here without the memory of you tainting it."

"Don't you think you are overreacting?" He sighs loudly.

"I don't, actually," I say. "I'm being very reasonable. I'm not even yelling at you. Which I do think you deserve for being a total fuckface." I sling on my heart-covered jacket, tuck my adorable, impractically tiny, date-night purse under my arm, and leave.

I can't believe I agreed to go out with this guy. A misunderstanding about a date is one thing, but, as usual, I'm better off alone. People always find a way to disappoint you. I don't know why I thought this time might be different.

It was almost a twenty-minute walk here—not a big deal to head back, even on an empty stomach—but two blocks from the restaurant the rain starts and immediately becomes a torrential downpour. The water hits me like a sheet, and in a few seconds I'm soaked to the bone. With another twelve blocks to walk, I duck into an alcove of the closest building to escape the drops. Maybe I can persuade my roommate to come pick me up or book a ride share app.

But my impractical purse holds up to its description. The zipper sticks, and when I finally jerk it open the contents spill onto the wet ground. My phone skitters across the sidewalk, stopping right on the edge of a large puddle.

I snatch it up, feeling sure I've rescued it from a wet grave, but the previously cracked screen now proves to be completely shattered. Trying to unlock it results in a still-black screen and a tiny laceration on my finger.

"Shit. Fuck. Balls," I mutter, sticking my pointer finger into my mouth to suck the pain away. I'm not going to further ruin the evening by getting blood on my cute outfit.

A black town car slows to a stop in the street beside me, the back window lowers and a male voice emerges.

"Do you need a ride?" the voice asks.

"No!" I blurt, without turning to look at my potential abductor. I'm not getting into a car with a stranger, not even one with a nice voice.

"It's raining, you are getting wet. It's really not a problem—"

I don't bother facing the car. I just flip my middle finger in his direction. "Fuck off, fuckstick." I don't say it too loudly. No point in pissing the guy off more than necessary.

"Seems a bit harsh, Ms. Thorn." The voice clicks into place in my memory. Only one person calls me Ms. Thorn with that kind of bravado.

I spin around to find Sacha Kwatch watching me from the backseat of the car. I flipped off my boss. I am still flipping off my boss. I drop my hand to my side.

"Mr. Kwatch, sir, I'm so sorry. I didn't know it was you—"

"Get in the car, Ms. Thorn. You can continue groveling when you are out of the rain."

The little command sends a pulse straight to my pussy. Fuck, I'm in trouble. Get into the back of the car with my hot boss who tries to fuck all of his assistants? Or stand in the rain like a fool and face the consequences of turning him down?

The door pops open.

I've probably been trapped in a car with worse. I release a deep sigh and climb into the backseat, sliding my wet ass across pristine black leather to sit beside my hot boss.

6

ENTIRELY INAPPROPRIATE

SACHA

I knew her silhouette the moment I saw it through my tinted car window. I couldn't just leave her stranded in the terrible weather.

Now, she's beside me, unbearably close, her warmth sinking into my thigh where our legs brush. Her forest scent invading my nose. She looks at me sheepishly through her dark lashes. She's wet, and vulnerable, like a defenseless doe alone in the woods, and in this flimsy outfit I bet I could have her completely unclothed in seconds. I could drag her across the seat into my waiting lap, tug up that skirt, finally find out what gets her pussy wet, have her begging me to cum inside her—

I crack open my window eager for a breath of untainted air to clear my head, and hope she doesn't notice that a small amount of rain slips in.

"I'm sorry, sir. I wasn't thinking. If I'd realized it was you, I wouldn't have—"

"Called me a fuckstick?" I finish for her.

"You heard that part?" She grimaces. "That wasn't really meant for you, sir. Obviously, I don't think you are a fuckstick. Or maybe it's not obvious, but I certainly

would like for it to be obvious." Her little nervous rambles are endearing. I think I like making her a little nervous.

"It's fine, Ms. Thorn," I assure her; she rewards me with a small smile, it's even nicer than the ramble.

"What are you doing in this part of town?" she asks.

"I was just heading to dinner." I'm not willing to admit I heard her mention her favorite restaurant the other day and wanted to try it myself. "You?"

"Leaving it." She takes a deep breath, her breast rising and falling under her flimsy wet top. She isn't wearing a bra tonight. I do not have to look hard to notice the exact size, shape and location of her nipples. I can't help wondering what they taste like. One quick tug is all it would take. She'd be totally exposed, I could have my mouth on her breasts in moments, and—

I tear my eyes from her chest.

"Special occasion?" I gesture at her outfit.

"It was supposed to be."

"You look nice."

"Please, I look like an absolute mess." She chuckles and wipes at the makeup smeared under her eyes. Shivering she tugs her light jacket tighter across her chest.

"You don't," I say. Her face softens just a little. "You look—cold." I shrug off my own jacket and drape it over her, hoping to remove a small amount of my temptation.

"Mr. Kwatch, I don't want to get your clothes wet." She protests lightly, but tugs the jacket a little closer. Putting her scent on it, putting my scent on her. My mate. A little shiver of excitement chases up my spine.

I wave my hand dismissively. "Where are you headed now?"

"Home," she admits.

"Where is that?"

"Please, don't go out of your way for me, sir."

My cock jumps every time she calls me sir. "I won't leave you stranded in this weather."

"Really. I can walk. It's just a few blocks from here, on Pine."

I pass the directions on to my driver. Bay gives me a soft smile, and my chest squeezes. I could easily slip my hand up her thigh, shove beneath that skirt, have her riding my hand until she—

My phone buzzes in my pocket—another notification, another email. I glare at the screen. Another inane work question. I type a quick clarifying response and press send before catching Bailey's eye again.

"Did yours survive?" I ask. She gives me a questioning look, and I point to the phone in her hand. "Being thrown across the sidewalk?"

"It wasn't thrown. I dropped it a reasonable distance." She sticks her nose in the air before glancing down with a scowl and admitting, "I don't think it survived. I can get a new one with my paycheck on Friday."

"Friday? I can give you a new phone now."

"I can buy my own, sir."

I shift my legs as my cock twitches. "I get them for free all the time." I pull an unopened box from the armrest of the car. "Everyone wants the owner of the largest computer security company to be seen using their phone."

"You can't do that." She seems surprised at the offer.

"I can. I never got a free phone handed to me when I actually needed one. People who get the most free stuff are usually the people who need free stuff the least."

She shakes her head. "I can't accept a gift from you."

"It's not a gift, it's a necessity. I need to be able to contact my assistant at any time. I need you available to me."

I press the box into her hands, her small fingers wrap around it.

"Thanks." Her lips turn up slightly. They are painted bright pink today. I briefly picture them wrapped around my cock before I manage to pull myself together again. Her scent in this small car is going to drive me to madness.

I'd give Bailey a new phone and a ride even if I wasn't madly in love with her. I would have done it for Mrs. Morton, or the assistant before her, or the one before him. Whatever their names were, I would have helped them if I'd found them stranded in a similar situation.

I'm not doing anything inappropriate.

Bailey's hand shifts on the seat between us, our fingers brush briefly, sending a jolt through my body that is entirely inappropriate.

Her blue eyes lock on mine. Maybe it's my imagination, but there's something more than just gratitude in that look. Can she feel the mating bond? I didn't think that humans had them, but—the town car rolls to a stop. She rips her gaze away, and the spell is broken.

"Let me walk you inside." I pull out an umbrella from under the seat. "Another benefit of being rich, someone else is paid to keep your car stocked with the essentials."

7

LARGE CAPABLE HAND

BAILEY

It's easy to forget how large Sacha is until all eight feet of him is standing behind you, holding an umbrella big enough to shield a family of five. He waits patiently while I fish my apartment key out of my purse.

Even though it's Saturday he's still wearing a suit; I wonder if he was in the office today or if he just dresses like this all the time. His dark blue suit jacket is tucked around my shoulders. He's wearing a neatly tailored white button-down, with a thin black tie. The guy knows how to dress himself, that's for sure.

His posture is excellent. He carries himself with the confidence earned from being a tall, handsome, self-made millionaire. Billionaire? I wonder how much money he actually has. His eyes flick down to mine, and I realize I might be staring. I flash him a quick grin. He gives me an easy smile in return. My stomach flips with delight.

And oh shit, I am in trouble.

I might want to have sex with my boss.

This is why I can't have nice things. Because I'm an idiot, who makes bad decisions, and falls for unattainable men. Of course I like him. I already know he's a bad guy who fucks his assistants and then fires

them. Or fires them when they turn him down? Which is worse?

All that matters is that I can't have a fling with my boss at the best paying job I've ever had. I have to keep it.

"Thanks for the ride, Mr. Kwatch." My fingers finally wrap around the cool metal key. "I'd love to invite you in, but—" I mentally catalog our dirty living room, the stained futon, the mismatched thrift store end tables, the scratched Ikea coffee table we found on the curb when our neighbor moved out, "I think I'm actually too poor to let you see how I live."

"I'm sure your home is perfectly acceptable." Sacha shakes his head.

"I doubt you'd say that if you saw it; I'm saving you from getting covered in cat hair—" I hurriedly open my door, hoping to get him out of my hair. Later, I can get him out of my head with a quick flick of the bean.

"Wait! Shit! Stop!" My roommate, Margot, yells as the apartment door swings open.

She's too late. A herd of tiny foster kittens swarms the entrance, mewling excitedly as they make a break for the terrifying freedom of the city streets.

Crouching, I manage to grab the two slowest escapees by the scruff. I swivel to capture the rest, but Sacha has easily scooped up the remaining three with one large, capable hand. He cradles the two black kittens close to his broad chest, while the little calico uses her tiny needle claws to climb his shirt, yowling the entire way to his shoulder.

Yep. I definitely want to fuck my boss.

"Shit, shit. Sorry, Cheddar! I'm so sorry!" Margot appears in the doorway with the sixth kitten in one hand and a wooden spoon in the other. "I didn't think you'd be home for hours. They can get out of their enclosure now. Did you know that?" Her words stop when she catches sight of Sacha, and her eyes trail from his bare toes all the way up to the top of his head. She smirks and pushes a strand of long brown hair behind her ear. "Who's this?"

"This is Sacha Kwatch. My new boss."

Margot's big green eyes widen. "Is this the coworker you went on the date with?"

"No." I shush her with a look before she can say anything else and scoot past her into the living room.

Rhapsody, the exhausted mama cat, gives my leg a brush hello before I set Galileo and Figaro down in the playpen that they previously couldn't escape. Figaro immediately begins to scale the side. Keeping them contained might be a thing of the past.

"You were on a date with a coworker?" There's an edge to Sacha's voice, probably because I'm already breaking some office fraternization rule I didn't know about, he shakes his head. "Don't answer that, it's none of my business."

I take the piebald Magnifico and the tiny black Scaramouch from his hands and put them with their siblings. Beelzebub is clinging desperately to his shoulder, leaving little pulls in the fabric of his nice shirt.

He extracts the kitten from his person gently, scratching under her chin with one large finger. The little daredevil purrs for him. Rhapsody weaves between his legs. He stoops to run his fingers along her back and return her kitten.

Margot watches all of this with her lower lip tucked between her teeth. "This is the guy who said you smell bad?"

"Margot, please!"

Sacha winces. "You don't smell bad, Ms. Thorn. Sorry if that was implied. Bigfoots just have an...intense olfactory ability."

"You gave Cheddar Bay Biscuit a ride home?"

"I saw Ms. Thorn on the street while I was headed to dinner," Sacha says. He's still petting the foster cat, who's rolled over to show him her belly.

"Right. Of course you did."

"I got caught in the rain," I say. "It was very nice of him."

"Clearly." Margot eyes the large jacket that engulfs me.

I start to shrug the coat off, regretting that I have to give it back. It's warm and it smells like him. "Sorry, if it's covered in cat hair now."

"It's not a problem." He holds out the new phone.

"What's that?" Margot points her wooden spoon at the box. "Did you finally get a new phone? Did he buy you a new phone?"

"It's for work." It's a small lie and when I glance at Sacha hoping he will confirm, I catch his eyes skirting across my unsupported tits again, the way he did in the car. I roll my shoulders back, trying to present the girls in their most flattering position. It should be irritating for your boss to ogle you, but right now I only feel slightly complimented.

"Well, I hope you stay and help her set it up, because, after the last one, I am not spending hours trying to teach this Luddite how to transfer her information. Do Bigfoots eat chili?"

He blinks at her.

"I'm making vegetarian chili for dinner. I thought I'd be home alone for the evening, but there's more than enough for everyone. I assume you didn't eat either, Bay, since you are home early."

"You assume correctly," I mutter.

"I couldn't possibly impose," Sacha says.

"Not an imposition. I offered it up!" Margot waves her spoon through the air.

"Margot makes good chili. You should stay," I find myself saying, "If you want," I hurriedly add, realizing a billionaire doesn't need to slum it in his assistant's grimy apartment. I turn toward the hallway to my bedroom. "I'm just going to change out of these wet clothes."

I escape down the hall to my bedroom, where I stare at my wardrobe for a long time, trying to decide what to wear. Nothing too revealing. Nothing too cute. Something comfortable, but not *too* comfortable. My favorite leggings are so threadbare you can see my ass through them, but I don't think that's what I want to expose him to tonight. I need to remove all sexual tension from this situation; it will ruin everything if I try to fuck him. I pull an old pair of Christmas pajamas from the bottom of my drawer. The safest bet. Baggy red flannel, with reindeer leaping across them, definitely does not say 'Please try to sleep with me, big sexy boss man'.

Fully dressed, I return to the living room to find Sacha sitting on the carpeted floor, his back leaning against the cat-hair-covered futon, half a dozen kittens clamoring across his lap, and one large hand idly stroking Rhapsody, who is already completely in love with him.

Good taste, that cat.

"What's her name?" He grins up at me, his whole face melting into something alarmingly attractive. He looks, actually—happy.

I may have been too hasty when I chose my outfit.

"Rhapsody," I say. "She's a foster, just staying here until she finds the right place to live forever." I crouch

beside him, and his nostrils flare as I point to the kittens. "Galileo, Figaro, Magnifico, Scaramouch, Fandango, and you already met Beelzebub. You like cats?"

"It's uh...a Bigfoot thing. Animals tend to love us. I usually love them back." There's a quiet contentment on his face.

"You have any pets?"

He shakes his head. "Grew up with some, but since moving to the city, I haven't taken the plunge. We moved around a lot with the start-up, but now that I'm settled, I've thought about finding a friend."

"Rhapsody and her kittens will be available soon. Some already have homes lined up, but I foster all the time, so if you have any questions, you can ask me."

"I will." His voice hits a low pitch that unsettles my stomach.

Margot is humming something in the kitchen, and that makes me far too aware of being completely alone with Sacha. Aware of the way his thick dark eyelashes flutter on his cheeks, the way his broad shoulders move under his shirt. He's rolled up his shirt sleeves, exposing more inches of muscly hairy arm; the long red fur at his wrist snakes up his forearms to disappear under his shirt.

I wonder how much more hair there is. Does it stretch all the way up his broad shoulders? Does it cover his wide chest? How hairy is his back, or his ass? Or his dick? He's a big guy. I bet his dick is big too. I try to ignore the urge to look at his lap, but my eyes naturally fall there.

And then I notice the phones in his lap. Two phones. My broken one and the brand new one. Panic wells up inside of me.

"Are you going through my phone?"

"I gave him your passcode. I don't have the patience to help you with it again!" Margot calls from the other room.

"I'm just moving your data to the new one."

"There are private things on there." I scowl in my roommate's direction.

"You don't have anything he shouldn't see."

"There are certain things he definitely shouldn't see, Margot."

"Whoops. Forgot about the photos." Margot feigns innocence, but she is a scheming two-faced liar who did this on purpose.

"Photos?" Sacha asks, and then his face blanches, like it hadn't even occurred to him that my phone might contain private information, private photos. His eyes drop to the devices in his lap. "Oh! I didn't see anything! I didn't look for anything! I wouldn't! Confidentiality is a cornerstone of the Cryptech company!" He coughs and hands me the new phone. "You should be all set up."

"It's okay, I trust you," I say it on instinct, but am kind of surprised when I realize it's true.

"Trust is a vital quality between employers and their employees." He gently dislodges the kittens from his lap and stands to his full height.

"Are you leaving?" I didn't really think he would stay, but I'm still a little disappointed to see him go.

"I have places I should be. Please tell your friend that I appreciate her offer." He's already retreating toward the door, his attention back on his own phone screen, but he looks up and gives me a smile before he opens the front door.

"Thank you, sir. For the ride. And the new phone." I start wrangling kittens as my boss closes the door, leaving my small apartment.

"Is he gone?" Margot's head pops into the room a moment later. The latch has barely closed before she is asking, "You are going to fuck him, right?"

"Margot," I hiss.

She just grins. "I would fuck him if I were you, is all I'm saying."

"Yeah. Obviously, you would. You're a whore." I toss a throw pillow in her direction.

She laughs. "I'm not a whore, Cheddar. Whores get money. I'm just a poor law student who sleeps around!"

"I don't think he wants to sleep with me."

"He definitely does," she counters.

"Probably," I admit. We both saw him staring at my tits then. I scrunch my nose. "I think he fucks a lot of his assistants, and none of them have lasted very long. I need this job, Margot! It's such good money. If I play my cards right, they might actually hire me full time! I won't have to keep being a temp."

"But if you fuck your rich boss, then maybe you will have a rich boyfriend *and* a job!" Margot grins wildly.

"I'm trying really hard not to fuck it up this time." If I make this last, then I can finally put my business degree to good use. I can follow my real dreams. I can find a way to make a difference in the world.

"I know, babe." Margot's face softens. She's my oldest friend; she's stuck by my side through every whim or wild idea I've ever attempted. "Chili?"

I happily follow her into the kitchen. Margot is my ride or die. Since we met our freshman year of college, and beautiful, talented Margot's life has always gone swimmingly. She's got an excellent GPA, a killer internship, and she's about to start her last year of law school.

Meanwhile, I finished my MBA thirteen months ago and am still floundering to find my footing. Margot's always supported every odd idea I've had, until each of those plans failed out. I've feel like I've been jumping from one job opportunity to the next, but it's hard to stand still when bills and debt make the world feel like it could crumble out from under you at any moment. The only thing I can seem to commit to is helping animals find people who love them.

Too bad toe beans can't be used to pay rent.

I need to make this job last. I'm not going to fuck up and get fired, I'm not going to run away at the first sign of trouble, and I am not going to sleep with Sacha Kwatch.

8

HOT PASTRAMI

SACHA

It's almost 9 PM, and I'm sitting in my office, staring at a pile of documents, again. The dry recycled air from the AC rattles in my chest. I loosen my tie.

"Just take it off," Ness grumbles. "There's no one left in the office to see you in mild disarray."

I scowl in his general direction. He doesn't take his eyes off of his laptop screen.

"We wouldn't be here if I'd just worked last Saturday," I mutter, but then I wouldn't have seen Bailey's home, met her cat, or her roommate, or learned anything about her life.

Ness and I have been hashing out the final details of this presentation for far too long. The office has been empty for hours, it's only filled with the colorful rays of the sunset through the wide windows, when an unexpected knock comes from my office door.

"Who is it?" I snap, irritated at being disrupted.

"Sorry for the interruption," Bay says. "It's only me, sir."

Dammit. I love it when she calls me sir.

"Ms. Thorn, you shouldn't be here this time of day. I thought you went home hours ago." I glance to the door, she's cast in the golden rays of the setting sun. How does she always look so beautiful?

Ness finally looks up from his computer, stretches his arms, and leans back against his seat to get a better view of the scene.

"Midnight oil, sir. If you are staying late, I thought I could catch up on some work, and be here if you needed anything." Bailey steps into the office with a small smile on her lips. She's painted them bright red today.

"I'm sure I could think of something Sacha needs." Ness curves his long neck to watch me. I could kill him.

"That was thoughtful, Ms. Thorn, but we don't need anything." I manage not to say that I need her to scream my name while I'm inside her.

"Well, I thought you might need dinner?" Bay holds up a brown paper bag that smells like heaven.

"Food?" I grumble at the same time that my stomach does.

"Just a bagel, with cream cheese and lox."

I sniff the air. "Toasted?" I don't know which smells better, the food or her.

"Of course. You always get it toasted." She smiles lightly.

She remembers my order. I could kiss her.

I really want to kiss her.

"What did you bring for me?" Ness asks with a smirk.

Bay turns to him in surprise, seeming to realize he is there.

"Sorry, I didn't think...Can I get you something, Mr. Loch?"

Ness watches her with a heat in his eyes that makes me furious.

"Thank you, Ms. Thorn." I step between Bay and Ness to block his view, my hand out to retrieve my dinner, pausing just as I wrap my fingers around the paper bag. "How did you get this?"

Her nose scrunches. "It was just a quick ten minutes to the deli across the street. I didn't think you'd mind if I took a break. I was getting something for dinner for myself; I thought you might want something too."

"Don't do that again." I pull back my empty hand and move toward my desk.

"Sorry, sir," she says quietly, "I didn't think you would mind if I took a quick break for food. I just got carryout. I'm going to eat it at my desk—"

I jerk open my desk drawer and pull out the envelope for discretionary funds. "Ms. Thorn, you aren't in trouble, but you shouldn't be using your personal money to buy me food."

I cross the room and replace the bag in her hand with my credit card.

"The company makes allowances for these types of purchases. Please, in the future use this."

"Oh! Okay. Certainly, Mr. Kwatch." She smiles softly and meets my gaze, her blue eyes glittering. I wonder if she likes to make eye contact when she gives head. I'd love to see her look up at me like that with my cock in her mouth. "Please, let me know if I can do anything else."

"Well, if the Amex is on the table," Ness says, "then order us dinner from Nobu."

"Is that...what you want me to do? I can find the phone number, or—" she asks, seeming confused.

"Don't indulge him. Just get him a sandwich from the deli too."

"Hot pastrami," Ness says begrudgingly. "Extra pickles."

"Absolutely." Bay hurries from the room, her hips sway in a pair of pants that perfectly hugs her ass. I long to wrap both hands around that ass, spread her legs, and sink into her.

"Was that the company black card?" Ness asks when the door closes behind her.

"She's my assistant. She needs to be able to purchase things for me."

"You gave your other secretaries access to the company card?"

"None of my recent assistants have lasted long enough to justify it," I mutter.

He snorts before turning back to his computer.

"She passed all the background checks we ran. I don't see a problem with it." The company has strict security protocols to eliminate any possible ties to certain competitors, or some of our customers' competitors.

"Not a problem! I just love how clueless you can be." He moves his computer from his lap before he stretches his long legs wide.

"Clueless about what?"

"The crush situation." He waves his hand through the air gesturing to the room in general.

"I'm not interested in her." I scowl, not wanting to rehash this argument with him. I don't want to talk to Ness about fated mates, not when his rejected him years ago.

"I mean the lass." He grins slyly. "She likes you."

"No—" I spare a glance to the door to see if it's possible she heard. "Do you think so?" I've had a few human girlfriends. Some humans certainly don't mind sleeping with cryptids, and this woman, who is meant to be mine, might be one of them?

"Oh, mister boss man, I just thought you might be hungry..." Ness mocks in a breathy voice, fluttering imaginary eyelashes at me.

"You're being ridiculous." Unless he's right. I'd love for him to be right. I can't stop fantasizing about her. My cock is getting tired of the constant self abuse it's received when I think of her.

"She's different than the other females you've dated. The human women or the other ones," he says. "I like it. I think it's good for you."

"Different how?"

"First of all, she's not some stuck-up rich kid," he mutters. "She's actually nice."

"She's too nice," I say. "She wouldn't like dating a monster." She won't appreciate the things I want to do to her. There's a driving need inside me to rut her like a beast—to claim her, knot her, chase her through the woods and ruin her for anyone but me.

"Pft," Ness dismisses me, "don't underestimate nice girls. They can get wild too. Give her a chance."

If only it were that simple. Bailey is the only one for me. I will only get one chance, I have to be sure not to fuck it up. I just hope I can keep it together long enough to wait for the perfect opportunity.

9

HE'S A BEAST

BAILEY

Almost four weeks have passed since I started this job and I haven't gotten any better at it. The hours are way longer than I expected. Sacha loves to stay in his office well into the evening, which means I'm staying in the office until well into the evening too. It's annoying at times, but at least my bank account is starting to look a little more flush.

I haven't gotten any better with Excel. It should be simple, it's just numbers in little boxes, but the program never quite does what I want it to do. I've already been told to stop sorting columns. But honestly, what are they there for if I'm not allowed to sort them?

Everything important has disappeared for the third time today, and Tatiana sighs a little louder each time I ask her for help.

"Ms. Thorn," Sacha appears in the doorway to his office, "I need the notes from yesterday's meeting."

"Of course, sir," I mutter.

"This is the third time that I've asked for them." His eyes flash to Tatiana. "Is this a social visit? Ms. Thorn is behind on her work."

"No sir, sorry. She's helping me with this spreadsheet." I come to Tatiana's defense.

"Again?" he asks, but waves away my answer before I can form it. "Just get me the notes once Tatiana has fixed whatever needs to be fixed."

"Right away, sir. Sorry, Mr. Kwatch, sir," I say. "I just need to type them up."

"You haven't typed them yet?" He raises an eyebrow.

I physically wince.

"It's fine, just, I need them as soon as possible." His fingers drum along the door frame and takes a deep breath. "Can you add a meeting to the calendar? I need to see you in my office. Set it for four-thirty tomorrow, please."

"Four-thirty on a Friday?" I squeak.

Tatiana gives me a beleaguered smile. We both know what a late meeting on a Friday means.

"I have some spare time then, don't I?" Sacha asks.

I swallow hard. "Yes, sir."

He nods curtly and ducks back into his office. There's a sour taste in my mouth. I've been here before. A meeting last thing on a Friday? I'm going to get fired, for sure. I've done nothing but fuck up since I took this job.

I need this paycheck. It's the best-paying gig I've had since, well, ever. I can't lose it now.

"Yikes." Tatiana shakes her head, her green dreadlocks moving almost like snakes. "That doesn't sound great. Sorry babe, I'm honestly surprised you lasted this long."

"Excuse you?" I scoff. Despite my ineptitude with Excel, I thought Tatiana and I were becoming friends.

"I mean," she laughs at me in that way she can where it doesn't feel like the joke is at my expense, "I can't believe you put up with him. I've heard he does some disgusting things behind closed doors. The women who worked here before you told me some gross stories."

"They did?"

"Surely you have some horror stories of your own?" she asks.

"Not really," I venture.

"Ugh, I guess you are one of the lucky ones. Personally, I make sure never to be alone in a room with him."

Gross stories. Pretty obvious she's talking about propositioning his employees. Sure, hitting on your assistants is wrong. It's totally inappropriate, it'd make him a monster to hit on people who depend on him for a job.

But I don't completely hate the idea of 'working' under him, or working bent over his desk, or working up against a filing cabinet. I'd work with him all night long.

"He hasn't seemed that bad," I say, thinking about the kittens, the new phone, the jacket. Yeah, he's stared at my tits a couple times, but it's probably fewer times than I've ogled those wide shoulders, or those big hands, or the way he rolls up his shirt sleeves when things are getting serious.

Tatiana moves the mouse and clicks a button that I swear I've already clicked about seven times, and everything in the spreadsheet fixes itself. "There," she says with a sad smile, "and good luck, with whatever it is he wants to see you about. Maybe it's nothing, but if you do get fired, Jacob and I will take you out and get you so drunk you won't even remember that you lost your job."

"Thanks." I chew on my lower lip. I need this job, but would I really sleep with my hot boss to keep it?

When 4:30 on Friday rolls around, I'm still not sure what to expect. Sacha is either going to try to fuck me, or fire me. I feel certain of that. Even as I enter his office,

I'm not sure which I'd prefer. Or if it would be feasible. Am I good enough between the sheets to make up for how abysmal I am with spreadsheets?

For once in my life, running away from my problems might actually be the right decision.

When I walk into his office Sacha's back is to the door. I make sure to close it behind me so no one can hear us, whatever we'll be doing next. I plop into the chair across from his large desk.

"You wanted to see me, sir?"

He whirls around with irritation on his face.

10

ALONE TOGETHER

SACHA

"I didn't ask you to shut the door." I say it much louder than I intend and regret it immediately.

"Sorry, sir." Bay winces. She's already sitting in the chair in front of my desk. "I thought you wanted to speak to me in private."

"I do. It's just—" I shut my eyes. "It's been a long day." Dammit, I can't think like this. Every time she calls me sir my cock jumps, and her scent in the enclosed room is already assaulting me. I need a breath of fresh air.

I stomp across my office. I know I'm acting ridiculous, but I don't know how I managed to get through the last four weeks, and I don't know how much longer I can handle this. Being so close and unable to touch her is testing every ounce of control I have. The beast inside me knows I could have her squirming and moaning for me if I only gave in.

"Sorry. Sorry, sir," she repeats as she rises from her seat to watch me cross the room.

"Stop apologizing," I snap harsher than I should.

"I thought you'd want us to be alone, so other people couldn't hear—" her words stop suddenly and she watches me expectantly.

She looks absolutely delectable in a bright blue blouse and a green skirt that flares out at her hips. I could have her out of it in seconds.

"I think being alone together is a bad idea," I mutter.

"I don't mind being alone with you," her voice is whisper soft, "I kind of thought—you liked me too?"

The question in her voice breaks my heart. I pause with my hand on the doorknob, gripped so tight my knuckles are white. If I wasn't such a monster, I wouldn't hurt her this way.

"Of course I like you, Ms. Thorn. I never meant for you to think otherwise."

"Then what's the problem?"

"It's nothing."

"It doesn't seem like nothing," she presses. "If I'm doing something wrong, I'd like to know."

"You aren't doing anything wrong, Ms. Thorn. I'm the problem here."

"Really? Because if you just tell me what to do, I can do it. I need this job." Her hands fidget in front of her skirt before she fists them tight, and then puts them straight at her sides as she faces me. "I'll do anything to keep working here, sir."

"It's the way you smell," I blurt out, and my chest already feels lighter. "I need the door open because I have a hard time thinking when your scent is everywhere."

"It's that bad?" she asks. I can't stop my gaze from roving over her body, the wide thighs begging to be tugged apart, the breasts straining at her blouse. I know what lurks under the fabric, I've glimpsed the dark nipples that wait to be revealed, sucked, and worshiped.

"It's the opposite of bad. It makes me think inappropriate things." My hormones swirling through my brain, muddling my logic. I need her so badly.

"What kinds of things?"

I shake my head. "Things that make me a monster, Ms. Thorn."

"What kind of monster?"

"Let's hope you never find out."

"I might be willing to—" she takes a deep breath, "—to find out. If you leave the door closed?"

The room is filled with her scent. She's mine, she is meant to be mine.

"I want you, Ms. Thorn. I want to know what you feel like wrapped around me. What every inch of you tastes like. What you look like spread across my desk—" The words spill out in a rush until my voice catches in my throat. It's wrong, but I can't contain myself any longer.

"This desk?" She rests her ass on the edge of the wooden surface. Her fingers curl around the lip, and she boosts herself up so that her toes barely graze the ground. Her skirt inches up her legs, showing more of that perfect skin.

I'm across the room before I know what I am doing. All I can think about is sliding my hand in between her legs, memorizing the dimples in her thighs, unbuttoning her blouse, taking her breast in my mouth, and every other phenomenal possibility once she's mine. I pause in front of her, memorizing the sight of her. Trying to imprint this moment before I've had the pleasure of really touching her. She wants me. It's there, written across her beautiful face, telegraphed in her body language, declared loudly in the rich scent of desire that settles between her legs. She leans back on my desk, she chest jutting temptingly forward.

I reach for her chin. Cupping her jaw in my thumb and forefinger. "Ms. Thorn—"

"I think Bay under these circumstances." A blush touches her cheeks. She leans ever so slightly into my touch.

"I shouldn't be doing this," I say so quietly I can barely hear it above the thunder of my heartbeat.

"Isn't that part of the fun, though?" She slips a finger under the lapel of my jacket to tug me closer. The light touch feels shockingly erotic.

"I'm a by-the-book guy—I do things the right way—I don't break the rules. I—"

"Is any of that going to stop you from taking what you want right now?" She cuts me off.

I suck in a breath before I lean down and brush my lips across hers, gentle and easy, with every ounce of restraint that I have left, trying not to frighten her. She gives a small gasp, almost like she's surprised by it. I keep going, savoring small presses of our lips against each other, indulging myself in the way she moves in response to me, enjoying the contest between our mouths. When I retreat, she presses forward, trying to pull more from me, but I stay at her mouth, letting the smell of her desire build between her legs as I seek out the taste of her. She parts her lips and lets me explore her deeper. Her flavor is as good as her smell—honey, moss, and spice. As I brush my tongue across hers, her hand flutters up, her nails digging into the back of my neck, pulling me in closer, tighter, hungrier.

Her other hand splays across the desk for support, knocking the folders from the surface as her legs fall further open, welcoming me. She presses her soft body up and into mine, those perfect breasts begging to be touched. I let a hand drift down, my fingers grazing across her tempting curves and valleys. She gives a soft sigh into my mouth, which urges me further. I dig my fingers into the folds of her hips as I move my lips down her neck to kiss the soft area above her clavicle.

Her hand fists into my shirt as her head tilts back to give me better access.

"This is all I have to do?" she asks so quietly I almost don't hear her.

"All you have to do?" I ask her neck, the lust in my brain barely makes room for thought.

"We do this, and I get to keep my job?" she asks.

I jerk back so quickly that Bay has to grab my arms to keep from losing her balance.

"No. No. I—" I shake my head, confused. "We do this, and then I get to keep you. As my wife."

11

HALF A MILLION IS A LOT OF CAT FOOD

BAILEY

Wife. Ridiculous. I laugh. "One kiss and you are proposing?" I tug his arm, trying to pull him back to me, but he leans further away.

"This isn't about your job, Bay."

"But—" My teeth wrap around my lower lip. "Isn't that why the other assistants left? Because they wouldn't sleep with you?"

"No!" He looks completely appalled. "No, no! I've never propositioned anyone at work." He moves even further away, my body is cold in his absence. "I thought you wanted this. I thought you might—dammit, I wasn't thinking at all."

My smile twists in confusion. "The others said—you know what, it doesn't matter. I misunderstood." I hop down from the desk and fumble to straighten my skirt, looking anywhere but at him. Fuck. I fucked up again. I kissed my boss. Yes, he propositioned me. Or did I proposition him? Fuck. Am I the one doing workplace harassment? "Am I still fired?"

"Fired?"

"You asked me here to fire me, didn't you?"

"No! I only called you in here to—it doesn't matter." His eyes search my face for a long moment. "I really like you, Ms. Thorn. I'm sorry. Your employment was never in jeopardy. I don't want you to feel pressured to do anything."

My heart melts just a little, and for some reason, I want to reassure him.

"I didn't exactly feel pressured. I practically threw myself at you." I try not to wince at the memory.

"I understand if you want to leave," he continues, like I haven't spoken at all.

"I don't want to leave," I insist. I need this job. He's not getting rid of me this easily. I can suffer awkward job situations for decent pay.

"Then I'll find a new position for you. I understand if you don't want to work for me anymore. The others didn't want to work for a monster either."

"It was just a kiss. You're hardly a monster," I mutter under my breath.

"I'm a Bigfoot, Ms. Thorn, you've noticed." He gestures to his body. "The other assistants left because they didn't want to work for a large hairy monster. I understand if you feel the same."

"Oh—oh." It's like the illusion shatters in my mind. "They meant a monster, literally! Like you are literally a monster. Like, literally, literally. That's why they are scared of you?" I laugh. He's practically a giant kitten. Nothing about him frightens me, except maybe the potential proposal. "I'm so sorry. I didn't... I'm not... I didn't mean it like that. I don't think of you as a monster."

"That has become apparent." His brown eyes scan my body, and my stomach flips.

"Can we just forget this happened? I'll go back to my desk. You won't need to find a new assistant, and we'll never speak of this again."

"No." He steps into the path between me and the office door.

"No?" I ask in a squeaky breath.

"Bay, I've wanted to kiss you since the first moment I saw you. I don't want to forget this happened. I want to be with you."

"You want to fuck me, you mean?" I laugh.

"I want you by my side every day, every moment."

"But you aren't serious, though." I shift on my feet, and suddenly it feels like the carpet is very interesting. My eyes search the berber for any kind of pattern.

"I like you, Ms. Thorn. A lot. I enjoy your company. You are clever, and funny, and kind, and sexy."

His feet appear in my line of sight. I look up to check his expression and am surprised by how close he's standing. He rewards me with a wide grin. He's so attractive when he smiles, and it's hard not to think about the way his strong hands traveled over my body.

Shit. I need to pull myself together. These things never work out. I'm a desperate idiot for even considering he might be telling the truth.

"Let's go out. On a date." It's a command, not a question.

"I can't date my boss."

"Can't date? But, you are willing to fuck me on my desk?" He cocks his head to one side.

"It's different." I scowl. "You know it's different. There are complications—expectations—"

"I'm crazy about you."

I bark out a laugh. "You barely know me."

"I want to get to know you."

I can't help that my heart gives a little flutter at that. "I need this job. I know I'm not good at it, but I need the

money. If we date, and you realize you don't want me around anymore—" My nose scrunches. "I have rent and student loans and—"

"What do you wish you were doing instead? As a career?" He cuts me off.

"Cat cafe." I say it without even thinking. "If I work here, for you, for a couple more years, I can maybe afford to open my own cafe."

"A cat cafe?"

"With coffee, and little pastries, and couches where you can sit and pet the cats, and a shelf with books by local authors, and craft parties that are cat themed, and I could make my own hours, and be my own boss. I volunteer for this non-profit that is always looking for forever homes for its pets, and I love helping the kittens find good homes—the right homes with people who will take good care of them—" I stop speaking, seeing the wide grin on his face. "You think it's silly."

"I think you are passionate, and it makes you even more beautiful."

His words do make me feel more beautiful. I close my arms over my chest and step away from him. I want to touch him again, which probably means I shouldn't. I have terrible instincts about these things.

"Let me be your business partner. Give you the capital to start."

"A business partner who wants to get into my pants?"

"It won't affect anything," he insists.

"It will affect everything." I bite back.

"I'll pay you then," he counters.

"What? To sleep with you?"

"To break up with me," he declares.

I laugh. "What does that even mean?"

"We date. When you decide it's over. I'll pay you."

I laugh again.

"How much are your student loans?" he asks.

"One hundred and twenty-seven thousand." I know the amount by heart. It's a constant weight on my shoulder, a number that hovers over me every day of my life. It's just another among the numerous dumb things I've done. I signed dumb loans. I delayed my graduation. I went to a pricey private school, expecting the prestige to help me land a job. (It hasn't.) I got myself into this mess with my stupid decisions and poor instincts.

"Five hundred thousand." Sacha interrupts my mental self-flagellation as he moves around his desk and slips into his office chair. He waits for me to respond, and when I only gape slack-jawed at him, he repeats, "I'll pay you five hundred thousand."

I laugh louder this time. Sacha's face remains serious.

"When you want to end it, I'll put the money in your account. Enough for your student loans, to start your cafe, and cushion yourself the first couple years, while you are in the red."

"Five hundred grand? Just like that?"

"I'm rich. It's not a big deal." He leans his broad forearms on his desk.

I shake my head. "You aren't serious."

"I am serious. I want you to have what you want, Ms. Thorn. And I can give it to you."

"And you want to fuck me."

"I want you to be mine. I want you *to want* to be mine." He steeples his fingers in front of his face, his voice lowering to a growl. "I don't want you working a job you hate, or feeling pressured to sleep with your boss to keep it. No matter how hot you think he is."

I bite my lip. "All I have to do is go out with you? Just once?"

"As many times as you decide, and when you don't want to spend time with me anymore, I'll transfer the money to you."

"What happens if you get tired of me first?" I ask.

"I won't," he says. "I'll never get tired of you."

"But if you do," I reiterate. Everyone gets tired of me eventually.

"You get the money," he offers. "When we break up, you get the money, No matter what."

There's a challenge in the silence that follows.

"Give me one date at least." He turns on his computer, his fingers flying across the keyboard. I lean around the desk to see his screen, just to satisfy my curiosity. He's filling out a contract with the details. "One date, and then you'll see I'm serious."

"One date? I'm just going to be the most expensive escort in the business?"

He shakes his head. "After one date, you are going to want another. I'm betting on it. I'm backing my bet with a half million dollars."

"Half a million." I repeat the number out loud, really acknowledging it for the first time. Half a million dollars is a lot of cat food. That's life-changing money, that could make all my dreams come true. "No strings? No loan? I just walk away with the cash?"

"It's all yours." He nods seriously. His brown eyes find mine and for a brief moment, I let myself indulge in the fantasy of him and me together. For longer than one date; getting to keep his big hands, his broad body, his soft lips.

"I pick our date. And I pay for it!" I blurt out. "No flying me to Paris, renting out the restaurant in the Eiffel

Tower, and claiming you already spent four hundred and ninety-nine thousand dollars."

"Whatever you want to do, I'll do it," he agrees.

"And when it goes badly or gets awkward, I walk away with the money? Like the world's easiest game show?"

"You get to walk away whenever you want. Keep your job, keep the money, keep my heart," he says, and my own chest squeezes.

"You're wasting your money," I say, steeling my nerves. "I'm not too proud to take it from you. I'm going to hold you to this."

"I expect you to."

I hesitate; watching him type. I have no idea if this would work. I want to do it, which means I probably shouldn't.

"Give me a copy of the contract." I gesture vaguely at his computer. "I'm going to show my roommate. She's a law student, she'll know if this is real." I lean over his shoulder to examine his computer screen. He smells alarmingly good, somehow like the sun is trapped in his fur, like a day in the park, sunshine, grass, and the best picnic you've ever had. The scent make me aware of how close we are. I jerk out of his personal space.

"I'll honor the deal," he promises, his eyes bright. "Have your lawyer friend look it over, and if she approves, we'll go out."

My chest feels tight. This is either the best idea or the worst idea I've ever agreed to. "Fine. Yes. It's a deal. It's a date."

12

IT ISN'T A DATE, IT'S A BRIBE

BAILEY

I rearrange the chopsticks beside my plate for the fifth time. I don't know why I'm so nervous. I've been to this restaurant a dozen times. I chose it because I know that I will have a good dinner, even if the night is awkward and terrible.

Not that it matters. This isn't a date, it's a bribe. I'm going to spend one evening with him, collect my money, and never see him again.

It's going to be so easy, so simple.

And then Sacha walks into the restaurant and I know for sure that I'm going to fuck everything up. Every head in the room turns to watch him stoop through the door. He's still wearing a suit. It's dark blue with white pinstripes and a little yellow pocket square in the jacket pocket.

He looks really good. Like, really, really good.

I wave before leaping to my feet. Sacha's eyes meet mine, and his face breaks into a wide, wonderful grin. His hand brushes my arm as he leans down to press a kiss to my cheek. My face heats at the light touch.

"You look beautiful." His gaze sweeps me up and down. "It's a nice outfit."

"Thank you," I wince.

Right, yes. The outfit.

It's an a-line royal blue skirt and a baby blue v-neck shirt. When I twirl you can almost *maybe* see my underwear. It's cute, it's flirty, it's got cleavage.

Margot insisted on helping me pick out what to wear. We spent almost two hours putting together the perfect outfit, one that looks like I put it together in two seconds. Now, my bed is littered with every article of clothing I own, which is fine, because I will not be taking my hot boss back to it tonight.

Letting Margot put it together was her reward for being my completely unofficial, and slightly illegal counsel, Margot reviewed Sacha's contract for me, but she could barely stop laughing at the proposal. She said it would never hold up in court, but Cryptech would probably honor it just to avoid the scandal of going to court. I have a copy of the agreement in my email, with a timestamp and everything. I might not get a half million dollars, but I would almost certainly get a payout if Sacha tries to back out of the agreement.

"You look really good too," I blurt out.

He glances down at his outfit.

"You always look really good. You are probably tired of hearing people say it," I add quickly.

"I don't get tired of anything you say."

"Corny." I poke him in the chest with one finger, flush a little at the contact with his hard chest, and decide to barrel the conversation forward. "But, it's obvious you put a lot of effort into your appearance."

"When people perceive you a certain way, an outfit is important. Clothes can make a man out of a monster."

"I think I understand that," I admit. Nothing conveys 'I don't care about your opinions on my weight', like bright colors that make you stand out in a crowd. "It's about not hiding the things society calls your flaws, and feeling comfortable in your own skin."

"You are perfect in your skin." He steps a little closer, not quite touching me, but I still feel warmth in my stomach.

"Are you hungry?" I ask, scooting into my seat. "I'm absolutely starving."

He settles into the chair across from me, his large body somewhat dwarfing the human-sized chair. "This is your favorite restaurant?"

"Yeah, I—How did you know?"

He picks up the menu, pretending to be engrossed in the list of sashimi. "I think I heard you mention it once." His eyes dart up to sheepishly meet mine. "When you were making a date with the IT guy."

"Right, Chris." I lick my tongue over my bottom lip, suddenly feeling nervous.

"Was that the date I found you leaving early?" He stares pointedly at the menu. "The night I gave you a ride?"

"It didn't go well." I don't miss the self-satisfied grin that glances across Sacha's face. "In fact, it was a fucking disaster."

He outright smiles at that. "I'm sorry. I mean, I'm sorry your dinner was bad that night, but I'm glad you're here with me instead."

I can't help but return his smile.

"How are the kittens?" he asks, and my heart squeezes that he cares enough to ask.

"Fantastic! We have a couple more weeks with them before they can be fixed, they all have forever homes lined up."

"Good." He smiles, and for a moment if feels like his eyes might bore through me. "And the mama cat?"

"Rhapsody?" I clarify.

"Does she have somewhere to go?"

"Not yet," I say, Sacha shifts in his seat, and a bright realization sparks through me. "Are you interested in adopting?"

"It's why I originally wanted to talk to you on Friday." He gives a sheepish smile.

"You weren't going to fire me, or fuck me—you were just going to ask about adopting the cat I am fostering?" My heart melts. I'm such an idiot asshole for assuming the worst.

"If you think it's appropriate? You aren't afraid I'm going to pull an A.L.F. and eat her?"

"Pull a what?"

"As long as you think it's safe to let a big hairy monster adopt an animal?"

I laugh lightly, but he doesn't smile. "There are people who'd think that wasn't safe?"

He shrugs.

"I think you'd probably be great at taking care of an animal." I can't look at him when I say it. "She'd be lucky to have you."

"You really think so?" His tone makes it seem like he isn't talking about a cat. Luckily, the server shows up and saves me from having to figure out how to answer that.

We order dinner, and it's delicious. Sacha is clearly pleased because he orders at least seven platters of the salmon sashimi. He apologizes to the waitress every time he asks for another one. My California roll and seaweed salad are great. Sacha only looks at his phone three or four times throughout dinner. It's hard to really blame him when he runs a huge company the way that he does.

But when I plant my credit card down beside the bill, I manage to get his full attention.

"I can't let you pay for everything," he says. "I ordered way too much!"

"I said this would be my treat."

"Let me leave the tip then." He pulls out his wallet and places several crisp hundreds on the table. It is the entire bill a few times over.

"Big tipper?" I think it's oddly sweet the way he quietly throws his money around, but this does seem excessive.

"I kept asking the server for more. I think she was irritated with me."

"You know you don't have to pay people to like you," I say with a laugh.

His eyes dart to me and then away. My stomach churns. I opened my big mouth and stuck my whole foot into it.

"You do that a lot? Give people money when you want them to like you?"

"I did it to you, didn't I?" he asks.

"Oh." I blink several times. "I didn't see it that way." I already liked him.

He doesn't speak while the server returns the bill.

"It won't come out of your payment, I promise." He slips the bills under the edge of his plate with a little smile that breaks my heart. The night could be over now. I've done my duty. He owes me half a million dollars. I can walk away right now.

"Let's make an agreement."

"We already have an agreement." He smiles.

"An amendment then. If you agree to put your phone away for the rest of the night and give me your

75

undivided attention, then I'll show you that I like you by spending a little more money." I offer him a smile.

"More time with you?" He shoves his phone into his pocket. "That sounds like a very agreeable deal."

13

WOULDN'T DEMEAN YOUR TALENT

SACHA

I slide my phone into my pocket, determined not to look at it again tonight. Work can wait. Bailey is right, I'm here for her, and she deserves my undivided attention.

I try not to let my undivided attention focus on how jealous I am of the small gold necklace that dangles in her cleavage, an area I am dying to explore myself.

"Can I ask you something?" She bites her lip as we exit the restaurant.

"Of course."

"It's potentially embarrassing, and maybe potentially fireable?" she continues.

"Color me intrigued."

"What does Cryptech do?"

I press my lips closed in an effort not to laugh.

"Sorry, sorry. It's just where the temp agency sent me, and I never really googled it. I just saw the hourly rate and said yes. I've rarely worked somewhere long enough to worry about what a company did, and obviously I know it's something to do with computers—" She rambles adorably, the way she does when she gets nervous.

My shoulders are shaking.

"Are you laughing at me?" she yelps. "Do not laugh at me! This is a real question!"

I shake my head. "I wouldn't fire you for not knowing what the company does. Although, I wish you'd asked me sooner. We build encryption software and computer security frameworks."

"See? See!" She pokes a finger into my chest. Heat blooms through me from the spot she touched. "I knew that you were going to explain with words that didn't actually clarify anything."

"You are right. We do computers." I shrug, tracking the movement of her hand as it leaves my body; she twirls in the opposite direction, her skirt flaring up, and giving a brief glorious glimpse of her thighs.

"Where are we going?" I call after her. "Should I order us a car?"

"We can walk!" She gestures for me to follow.

When I catch up with her at the crosswalk she looks up at me with glittering eyes. Her plump lips pull into a wide grin, and I can't stop thinking about the way they felt pressed against mine. Our knuckles graze, and she glances down at our hands. I take a deep breath before slipping her small fingers in between mine. I lose track of all the clarifying questions I was planning to ask when she squeezes my hand lightly. She drags me several blocks, to a small bar nestled back from the street. We show our IDs to the bouncer at the door of a bar. It's a little awkward getting my wallet out of my pocket with just one hand, but I don't have the heart to release her grip.

The bouncer takes a long time to size me up. I try to give him a reassuring smile. I'm used to this kind of treatment, and I don't really blame him. I wouldn't want anyone walking around my office who I thought might be a threat, and that's what cryptids are to humans. Potential threats. Usually, the suits help people see me as a human.

Eventually, he waves us through.

"The cover is a little expensive," Bailey tugs me inside. "But it's so worth it. Wait til you see the inside."

The building is dark, crowded, and filled with a cacophony of musical themes, chimes of bells, and the slam of plastic against metal. The ceilings are low, the room is dark, the building is long and narrow, with a wooden bar at the end. Both long walls are lined with pinball games. From older vintage models, to newer flashy machines.

"All the games are free to play. That's why they charge so much to get in." Bailey gestures to the rows of games. "It's kind of a great deal if we play for a while! Can I buy you a drink?"

I nod, feeling eyes track us as we cross the room. I know we make a strange sight. I'm used to drawing a certain amount of attention, but Bay barely seems to notice it. Her fingers squeeze mine tightly before she presses up to the bar and orders.

It's easier to lose her smell in this place, overwhelmed by the stale alcohol and the press of bodies. Hopefully, I'll be able to think about something that isn't how well her breasts would mold into my large hands.

She buys me a beer and herself a pineapple vodka and tugs me over to a Godzilla-themed machine. "Nice! It's available! This one's my favorite!" she gushes, pointing to the best aspects and explaining the nuances of a good table versus a bad one. She sets her drink into the holder beside the machine as she sets up a two-player game.

She promptly kicks my ass at it. My competitive side is furious, but I can't help but be proud that my mate is so talented.

"You're really good at this," I say.

"I was in a pinball club for a while. I joined a couple tournaments. Never got very far, though." She grins up at me. At this point in the night a slight glaze of alcohol shimmers in her eyes, with her inhibitions slightly lowered, she's all flirt. She leans in with one gentle hand on my chest, like she wants to tell me a secret.

I lower my ear so she can speak into it, taking advantage of the position to sniff her neck.

"You probably lost because you got distracted by my ass." She giggles, pulls back and wiggles the aforementioned body part.

"Not that it doesn't look excellent this evening, but I would never demean your talent by claiming such a thing." I slip a hand around her waist and dip to her ear. "Now if you were in that purple pencil skirt that you wore to work last Friday..."

"Scandalous, Mr. Kwatch!" She gasps in mock horror, but I keep my hand on her hip as she types her name into the scoreboard. 'BST'

"What does the S stand for?"

"Bailey, Samantha, Thorn." She ticks off her fingers as she says each name. She slides between me and the next machine in a way that presses her body against mine. "Because I am the best!"

"More like a little beast," I grumble when her breasts graze my arm. She laughs and gives me a little hip bump when I don't move out of her way quickly enough.

It's wonderful to see her really in her element. Giggling, having fun, and succeeding at something that she enjoys.

These are the moments my instincts must have scented on her. The beast inside me instinctively knew she was warm, talented, and full of passion.

But no matter how good she smells, nothing can compare to the teasing grin she flashes me as she pulls me over to another table, where I know she will destroy me again. I'm beginning to think that I could make this work. Really make it work. That my slow stalking of my mate is going to pay off, even if I did have to pay her to be here tonight, she's going to be mine very soon.

14

STINK LINES

BAILEY

The night is long. I know I'm not supposed to be enjoying myself this much, but it's easy to forget we aren't really on a date when he's so easy to be around. The evening is full of flirty glances and casual touches.

Sacha slips a hand along the back of my neck, heating up the sensitive nerves there as he leans in to compliment my pinball skills again. When his breath glances across my ear as he laughs at my joke, I almost have to excuse myself to find clean underwear.

He is dangerously sexy. I thought planning the date so soon would give me less time to get emotionally attached, but I don't think the plan is working.

When last call is announced, I'm surprised. I had no idea we'd been here so long. I down the rest of my cocktail and turn to find Sacha boring holes into me with his deep brown eyes.

"Are you ready to call it a night?" he asks, leaning toward me.

"I think so." My hands reach up unconsciously to straighten the lapels of his suit. "But first dates traditionally end a certain way."

"Oh?" he asks. "How's that's?" He lets himself be pulled toward me, surrounded by the lights and noise of the crowded bar, one of his large hands lands on the wall beside my head, and I squeeze my thighs together.

"Well, I probably wouldn't have even agreed to this date if you weren't such a good kisser." I force the words out. It's difficult to admit. I don't want him to get the wrong idea. I don't want him to think that I'm not going to take his money. He's cute, and nice, and is probably a good lay, but I'm not an idiot who walks away from a ridiculous sum offered by a rich person who has more than enough to spare. "This is probably your only chance."

"Alright, then. If I only get one chance, then I'd better make it good." His low voice rumbles through my entire body.

He traces a hand across my chin, his large thumb brushes across my lips, and shoots a heat straight to my stomach. His eyes sparkle in the arcade lights. For a second, even in the loud, crowded bar, everything seems still, like we are the only two people alive. He lowers himself to my face, and after a long golden moment of anticipation, he presses his lips to mine. Something sparks to life inside me, just like the first time we kissed. He is thorough, taking slow control of my mouth, claiming it inch by inch. There's no rush or urgency, just a solid, controlled power that he uses like he's trying to memorize the way our lips fit together. He's soft, warm, pleasant, and completely dominating with the intense strength I can feel under his skin. A heat spreads, like liquid chocolate, slowly across my body. I could melt into him and stay there all night.

His hand slides down, brushing knuckles against the side of my breasts, but even with my urging he doesn't take the kiss past PG. His hand comes to rest at my hip. I press against him, urging him to continue, to take things a little further, I want him to give in, take me home, and satisfy this itch I cannot scratch.

But he doesn't fold under pressure. I feel the smile in his kiss just before his teeth scrape over my bottom lip as he leans back. His hands leave my body to prop himself against the wall, caging me in with his arms. My body mourns the loss of him.

"Will you let me plan our second date?" He breath glances across my cheek.

I nod before remembering we aren't going to have a second date. Alcohol and his lips have lured me into a fuzzy state of intoxication. I'm going to break up with him on Monday and take his money. "What makes you think there's going to be a second date?" I ask, trying to recover, but making no effort to move away from him.

As an answer, his fingers wrap around my chin so he can guide my mouth up to meet his, pouring his warmth slowly back into me until he manages to pull a gentle groan from my chest. "I think you really want to know if I'm good at more than just kissing."

Dammit. Fuck. He's right.

"Give me one more week," he urges softly. Between his warm hand on my side, and the ache between my legs, I realize that I can wait another week for my money if I get a couple more tastes of this.

"One more date isn't going to kill me," I admit, and he rewards me with another long tender kiss before sending me home completely alone.

15

HE'S A BEAST

BAILEY

It's a lot easier to enjoy your job when you don't think your boss hates you. I still fuck up several times a day, but I'm a lot less nervous about being fired now that I understand my boss is just awkward because he wants to jump my bones, and in one more week, I won't have to worry about any of that anymore.

Work remains incredibly busy, which is a great distraction. The big contract Sacha has been working on all month is being finalized, and everyone is on edge all week. Still, every time he smiles at me, or puts his hand on my back, or says my name, it feels like my stomach might drop out of my body.

All three CEOs are in the office on Thursday. Mr. Pleasant's mostly nocturnal lifestyle means he doesn't keep normal office hours. He uses video conferences for almost all of his daytime meetings, so I've never seen the Mothman in person before. His large eyes are bright red in person, and his wide black moth wings look buttery soft. He's taller than I expected, almost as tall as Sacha, if you include the expressive antennae that wave above his head.

They keep the light-blocking shades drawn during the meeting so the light doesn't bother Mr. Pleasant's

sensitive eyesight, masking the room in shadows. I sit diligently at my bosses' side during the long boring meeting, proud of myself for resisting the urge to pull out my phone and play Merge Mansion. Sacha rotates his chair until his thigh presses against mine, and he leaves it there. The touch has the warmth of his body seeping into my knee. It brings a little heat to my cheeks and...other places. I shuffle nervously as the contracts are signed and notarized.

When it's done, there's a satisfied feeling in my stomach. I barely had anything to do with this project, but I know it's a load off of Sacha's mind, and it's nice to see his hard work pay off. I like the feeling of a completed task.

"We'll see you at Moonshine after work, Sacha?" Magnes asks as he steps toward the door. "We'll be putting the drinks on the company tab. I don't want you skipping it."

"I'll be there." Sacha reassures them, not moving from his chair.

I stand to follow the others, but Sacha motions for me to hang back as everyone else vacates the conference room. He gestures for me to step a little closer, and I lean against the conference table, shifting my armful of supplies—a laptop in one hand, my coffee mug in the other—so that I'm close enough to hear his quietly spoken words.

"Will you be joining us tonight, Ms. Thorn? Cryptech likes to make a show of appreciation to the staff after a big deal is closed. There will be an open bar for employees."

"I thought I'd come out for a couple of drinks."

"And are you still satisfied with our deal, Ms. Thorn? Or are you ready to extract yourself from the contract?" His eyes remain on the papers in front of him. So disinterested in me that, for a moment, I'm not sure which deal he is talking about.

I glance around the still dim, empty, conference room. There's no one else around, the door is closed, people passing through the hallway walk past the tall open windows like we aren't even here. We're alone now. It's the perfect chance to tell him I want to break up, to take his money, walk away, and never see him again. Never hear my name on his lips again. Never feel his hands touch me.

"I'm satisfied," I say quietly, then bite the inside of my cheek in frustration. Damn my hormones. That is not what I was supposed to say. "Unless you've changed your mind?" It occurs to me that this may be why he wanted to speak with me, until he looks me up and down with a gaze so heated that I could almost certainly complain to HR about it.

"No, Ms. Thorn." He tilts his body in my direction, his hand skirting across the conference table, stopping right beside the edge I'm leaning against. I stare at his hand as one long finger moves toward me and grazes against the outside of my thigh. He strokes gently up and down, fingering the fabric of my skirt. The almost incidental contact makes my whole body tense. "Do not anticipate me changing my mind about you. You wore the purple skirt again?" he asks.

"You did mention before that you appreciated it, sir—" My breath catches when I try to talk, and then my nerves have more words spilling out of me. "I bought it secondhand, I found it on a website that specializes in plus-size clothing, it can be really hard to find things that are work appropriate and fit me at a lot of normal stores, not to mention things that actually look cute, and fit in my budget."

"And it hugs that round ass like a glove." He stares at the place his hand touches my body, shaking his head slightly. "If I see you wearing this skirt to the office again, Ms. Thorn, I will not be responsible for my actions."

"What actions?" I ask carefully.

"I'll have no choice but to lock you in my office, bend you over my desk, and bury my cock in that sweet-smelling pussy." He growls.

"O—o—kay," I stutter out the syllables without thinking of anything except how much I would love for him to do just that.

"Okay?" he asks quietly. His chair rolls just an inch in my direction, and suddenly, I can hear my heartbeat in my ears.

The conference room door opens, the lights flick on unexpectedly. Sacha is already leaning away from me, his hands back to their appropriate place on the table in front of him.

"Sorry, Mr. Kwatch," a dark haired woman walks into the room, "I was sure we had the conference room scheduled at three today."

"Don't worry, we're leaving." Sacha says. "I was just clarifying a few items with my assistant. We can finish this conversation later, Ms. Thorn." He waves a hand in my direction.

I nod, unable to form a syllable. My mouth feels frozen closed, and I hurry past the people standing in the doorway, escaping to the relative safety of my desk.

16

CALL IN HUNGOVER

"Here! Shares!" Tatiana plops a tray of jello shots in front of us. Jacob reaches for two of them immediately, passing one to me. The pair have quickly become my best work friends. Tatiana always helps with my spreadsheet madness, and Jacob has all of the best office gossip. They are one of the better parts of my day, other than the occasions Sacha says my name.

Moonshine is a frequent after work hang-out spot. It's a laid back bar, just a few blocks from the Cryptech office building. The bar is partially owned by Mr. Pleasant, so it hosts regular company events. Apparently, being nocturnal means you have a particular interest in businesses that are open late.

"I'm not sure about jello shots." I need to keep my head. Across the room, in a slightly raised section of the bar, with plump leather couches and bottle service, sit the three chief officers. They share a couple bottles of fancy liquor amongst themselves. Magnes has his arm around a pretty blonde, and a disinterested dark-haired woman perches beside Pleasant. My Bigfoot is sitting gloriously alone. "Besides, we have work tomorrow."

"You've never been here when we finished a big project, but hardly anyone shows up to work after these things. If they do go into the office, they are hungover."

I shake my head.

"No worries. More for me." Jacob grins, pulling the little plastic container toward himself and swallowing the jello down down with expert precision.

Sacha briefly turns his big brown eyes in my direction. There's an unmistakable heat in that gaze as he takes a long sip of a dark brown liquid. Every part of my body feels aware of him, even though he's all the way across the room. When his gaze moves back to the other members of his group, it feels like I lost something.

"Has Mr. Kwatch ever propositioned any of his assistants?" I blurt to my companions.

"Not as far as I know." Tatiana grins wildly, the alcohol clearly fueling her courage. "Why? Did he say something to you?"

"No!" I say hastily, but my denial may have been too strong because she and Jacob share a smirk.

"Does the temp have a little crush?" Jacob asks.

"No. I just wondered why you all don't like him." I chew on my lower lip.

"Because he's a massive tool!" Tatiana exclaims.

"He's gross, eats smelly fish in the office, never wears shoes." Jacob visibly shudders. "I cannot stand seeing his bare feet everyday. He used to run to work. Can you even imagine? The whole office smelled like wet dog."

Tatiana begins listing things off on her fingers. "He's always grumpy, he's rude to everyone, and he loves yelling. Although, he's seemed less grumpy the past couple weeks." Tatiana nudges me. "Maybe your little crush has had a positive effect on the guy!"

"Not a crush." I repeat.

Tatiana snickers. "Sure it's not."

"Maybe I could have just one shot." I select a small plastic container from the tray, trying to change the subject. My co-workers cheer, each grabbing their own small, jiggly cup.

Our group parties well into the evening. The bar plays loud music, and the drinks are free-flowing. After a couple vodka pineapples I switch to just soda water and lime. I don't want a hangover tomorrow. My new friends do not seem to share that concern.

"Hey," I glance up from my text messages, "my friend, Margot, and her law school buddies are doing karaoke at a bar down the block. Do you want to come with me?"

"Hell yes!" Jacob yells.

"Absolutely!" Tatiana pumps a fist in the air. She chugs the rest of her drink, and twists in her seat, already heading for the door.

As we are leaving, I manage to catch Sacha's eye. He's leaning against a wall beside the hall that leads to the bathrooms. Now is my chance, I'm three drinks in, I can talk to him now. Tell him that I'm sure now, we aren't going to date anymore, I'm ready for my money.

"You guys go ahead." I tell my friends. "I think I left my cell phone at the table."

"We can wait for you." Tatiana offers.

"Maybe you should get Jacob out of here? Before he does anything he wouldn't want showing up in the office gossip?" I suggest with a grin.

"Let's go, I am ready to vocally express myself! I want to sing!" Jacob shimmies his hips, limbering himself up for an all-nighter.

"You are probably right, Bay." Tatiana smiles.

"Hurry, Bay! We are going to duet 'Suddenly Seymour'. You are not going to want to miss it!" Jacob yells over his shoulder as Tatiana slips a hand around his waist and guides him toward the door. They are already practicing some fairly impressive harmonies.

I turn, not to our former table, but toward the bathrooms. The hallway seems empty, and my heart sinks a little. Maybe I misread Sacha's meaning.

Then, a hand wraps around my wrist, tugging me into a dark corner of the hallway. I wish my body didn't welcome his touch quite so easily, but I relax into his embrace as his warm hands resting on my hips.

"Ms. Thorn." His low voice sends a pleasant little thrill straight through me.

"Mr. Kwatch." I bite back a little grin when I say his name. I haven't spoken to him all evening, but the few illicit glances across the room have me feeling warm all over. I have to pull back before this all becomes too much.

"Do you know how hard it is? To work beside you in the office every day and not be able to grab you? To touch you the way that I want to?" He backs me against the wall, his large frame towering over me.

"We aren't in the office, sir." There's a little challenge in my voice. I put a hand to his chest. It's a firm wall of muscle, I wonder how much of it is covered in hair.

"Someone could still see us here." He growls slightly.

"You haven't told them? Your friends?" I ask.

"No," he says. "You are my little secret, Bay. Just for me to enjoy. They wouldn't approve of the contract we signed."

"About our contract—" I swallow, hoping I can get the words out this time, but that hope dries up as Sacha's eyes search my face intently. He clasps my hand, keeping it pinned to his chest as he leans toward me.

I tilt my chin up, expecting a kiss, but his head veers to the side and his face presses into my shoulder. He inhales deeply, his breath tickling my neck on the way out. It sends a shiver down my spine to settle in the heat between my legs.

"Come away with me," he says quietly.

I laugh again. "You've been drinking?"

"No...Yes. It doesn't matter. I want to be alone with you, Bay." His quiet words make me squirm. "Let me take you away."

The fingers of his free hand dig into my hip, massaging the muscle there. His chest rises and falls beneath our clasped hands.

"Take me away?" I ask the question more for myself than for him, wondering what it would be like to let him control my life that way.

"What are you doing this weekend?" He cuts me off before I can answer. "It doesn't matter, cancel your plans. You are coming on a trip with me."

"You think I'll follow your orders?" I ask. "Just like that?"

"Tomorrow. 10 AM." He ignores my protest.

"We have work."

He shakes his head. "Call in sick. Your boss won't care, he won't be in the office."

"You can't order me around this way, Sacha."

"Pack warm. We'll be staying in the mountains."

"I am being serious, sir." I stiffen under him.

He pulls back to look me in the eye, and a small growl escapes the back of his throat. "It drives me through the roof when you call me sir."

There's a gleam in his eye that makes my knees weak. Still, I shake my head at him.

"I am leaving for the weekend." His voice gentles. "Magnes insists that I take some time off, and I want to spend a couple nights alone, in the mountains, disconnected from everyone. No phone, no internet, no work, no news." His fingers flex on my hip. "I don't know if I can be away from you for that long. I want you to come with me. I want to be with you."

"Then you won't be alone," I tease.

"We'll be alone, together." He smiles.

The request makes my chest tight, my mind reeling with the options as he lowers himself slowly, until his lips meet mine, and he presses a warm kiss into me. His mouth firm and insistent as his tongue delves forward, large and hot. I give him an encouraging little moan and try to tug him closer, but like every other time he's kissed me, his powerful hands barely scrape my body, skirting the areas with true intention, keeping his machinations a tease that drives my body wild with expectation. I need him to grab me, to take me, to drop his restraints and show me what all that bottled strength can do.

Sacha breaks the kiss as a server from the bar passes us. Pulling away from me quickly, he forces his back to the opposite side of the hallway.

"Please, come with me," he says. "Give me the weekend, and if you still aren't sure about us—about me—then we can end the contract. I'll leave you alone. I won't ask you for anything else."

"One weekend?" I try to ignore how heavily I am breathing.

"Two nights. I just want to be with you," he says. "Meet me tomorrow morning."

Every inch of my body wants to agree, which means that I probably shouldn't go. "Okay." I nod. It'll be one last little treat before I tell him goodbye forever, take my money, and run.

"I'll let you know where to meet me." He gives me a fleeting smile, his eyes are still drinking me in. Part of me almost feels guilty for taking advantage of him. One small date, a weekend away in a fancy mountain retreat. That's all I have to do to get half a million dollars.

"Text me the address." I concede.

"Is that a yes?"

"I should go. I need to meet my friends," I say as I turn to leave.

"Is that a yes?" he calls after me, a broad smile on his lips.

I run from the bar before I can answer.

My mind is still reeling when I reach the karaoke bar. Tatiana and Jacob are already in full swing, merging easily with Margot's law school friends. which gives me a few blessed moments alone to stew in my thoughts, stirring my drinking straw in my third pineapple vodka off the evening.

Margot sidles up next to me. "Big thoughts, Cheddar Bay Biscuit?"

"What?" I ask.

She presses her finger gently between my eyebrows, and I become aware of the crease there. I smile at her, trying to relax my expression, and, while my coworkers sing an absurdly long eight minute duet, I explain the situation to Margot.

"Do you think it's possible that he actually really likes me?" I ask.

"Of course he does. What's not to like?"

I roll my eyes, and Margot laughs before attempting to sober her face.

"Sweetie, he offered you half a million dollars to date him, he's taking you away for the weekend on your second date."

"So, you think I should go?" I feel the crease re-form between my brows.

"I think you should absolutely go." Margot giggles with glee. "You like him."

"No." I shake my head.

"Bay, it's okay to enjoy yourself. You are even allowed to like him."

"I don't," I mutter. "I mean yeah, he's nice, rich, hard-working—"

"Hot." Margot adds with a grin.

"He's my boss. I—" I chew on my lip, "He's paying me to date him...it would be so stupid to fall for him, and Margot, I'm tired of being stupid."

"You aren't stupid," Margot assures me.

"I do a lot of stupid things," I mutter.

"You take chances! You have passion! You are always trying new things!"

I'm always losing jobs. Jumping from one career to another. Always being too excited, or too stupid, or too much. Sacha inspires me that way, he seems so grounded, so sure of himself and what he wants from life. I find it hard just to stand still when it always feels like the ground is slipping out from under me.

Margot smirks, turning as my friends re-join our table, she asks them, "Have you ever dated someone you work with?"

"Jacob and I are just friends," Tatiana says quickly.

"I'm not really interested in women, and she is *very* interested in women," Jacob laughs, and I think I see a little blush rise up Tatiana's face.

"How does Cryptech feel about coworkers dating?" Margot asks.

"Well, I know I love talking about it," Jacob says.

"I think fraternization is fine?" Tatiana interjects. "As long as they don't work directly under each other, you know?"

"Why?" A wide grin splits Jacob's face. "Have you got your eye on someone, Temp?"

"No!" I say, far too quickly and too loudly not to be suspicious.

"No. My little Cheddar Bay Biscuit is too smart for an unrequited crush." Margot steps in, and I'm forever grateful for her cool demeanor. "I'm the one who can't stop thinking about one of my classmates. She won't even look in my direction." Margot throws an arm around Tatiana, pointing into the crowd to create a distraction that takes the heat off of me. She really is the best friend a girl could ask for.

I cannot let my gossipy coworkers find out I'm taking a long weekend with my boss, but the threat of our tryst being discovered isn't enough to stop my smile when my phone dings with a message. It's from Sacha. A short, three-line message. An address.

17

STINK LINES

SACHA

It's 10:17 AM when Bailey finally shows up at the airfield. I know because I've been obsessively checking my watch every ten to thirty seconds. My heart skips a beat when I finally see her bright pink hair shimmering in the morning sun. Despite her frequent text message assurances, I was beginning to think she wouldn't actually show up.

"Sorry, I'm late. Sorry!" Bailey yells as she approaches, her feet moving quickly, but not quite at a run.

"Was the car I ordered late?" I ask with a frown.

"No," She admits sheepishly, "it wasn't the car, it was me. Is this an airport?"

"A small one."

"I didn't make us miss the flight or anything did I? Are we getting on a plane?"

"Not a plane."

"I'm so sorry for being late. I hope I didn't worry you. I got home late last night, so I had to do a lot of packing this morning, and I know I over packed." She gestures to her large luggage, its zipper straining to contain the contents. "It's just two nights, but I wasn't

sure where we'd be going or what we'd be doing, so I didn't know what to bring. I had a hard time paring it down." She starts to ramble, a trait I am quickly growing fond of. "And then, I didn't want to be unprepared, and I wasn't sure about my hair, or makeup, or—"

I bend down and stop her nervous words with a light kiss to her lips, taking the chance to casually sniff her comforting scent. "That's my fault," I say as I pull away. "I didn't give you any details about where we were going. Of course you should have everything you need. You look beautiful," I add. She's wearing a pink leopard print sweater, and a pair of leggings that I cannot wait to see her turn around in.

"You always say that." She rolls her eyes before she breaks into a small smile. "You look nice, too. I like seeing you out of a suit."

It's just a black Henley and a pair of blue jeans, but I still preen under her compliment. "Are you ready?"

"Not sure if I can answer that, if we're not taking a plane."

"I'll show you." I slip one hand into hers, pick up her oversized luggage with the other, and tug them both toward the tarmac and the waiting helicopter.

"Are you freaking serious?" she asks.

"You aren't scared of heights, are you?" I ask, realizing I may have made a mistake. "It takes forever to get to the mountains in a car on the weekend."

"No! It's great—" She laughs. "I guess we'll just have to listen to my carefully curated road-trip playlist later."

I squeeze her hand and help her strap into one of the seats. In a few moments, we are high above the ground, the city fading from view as we head into the mountains. It's almost impossible to have a conversation in the helicopter, but I enjoy the way Bay wiggles nervously as she watches our trip from the window.

Sudden unease form a pit in my stomach. I hope she doesn't mind this trip. I've been so convinced she's meant to be mine it didn't even occur to me to warn her where we were going. When the helicopter lands in an empty field about a mile from my parents cabin in the woods, I'm more than a little nervous.

"You don't need to carry that. It's heavy," Bailey protests as I pick up her oversized luggage.

"Please. It's nothing," I say. "Besides, it's a mile walk, and you don't need to carry your bags when I can do it for you."

She bites her lower lip in an alarmingly alluring way. I don't know how I would live without that lower lip. I am going to have to make the most of our time together, to convince her to stay with me forever.

She follows me down the narrow trail into the forest. I've always found the woods I grew up in calming. Only a few moments of being dwarfed by giant trees, and my neck muscles already feel more relaxed. The fresh air in my lungs makes my chest lighter, and the echo of city noise dissipates from my ears. After a few twists in the trail, we approach the small red cabin with blue shutters.

"Is this where we are staying?" She sounds surprised.

"The whole weekend." I turn to see the confused expression on her face. "Is it that bad?"

"No! It's adorable, really! I just—I expected something—else." She shrugs.

"A chateau?"

"A turn-down service and a day spa, to be honest," she laughs, "But this is great. It's really sweet. Really." Her voice lowers a register, and I know she's being genuine.

"I should have explained better. I grew up here."

Her gaze scans the tall trees, taking in the seclusion, the absence of any sign of civilization, before she skeptically asks, "This is the childhood home of a tech magnate?"

"Humble beginnings and all that." I say. We cut through the yard, passing the old fire pit with hand-carved benches around it, the untended remnants of my mother's vegetable garden, and the rope swing they pushed me on when I was little. The place is full of cozy memories of my childhood.

We step up on the covered porch, and it still feels like home. The uneven wide-planked floors, the familiar scent of the wood burning stove in the corner, and our well-used kitchen table with a few handmade chairs surrounding it. There's a couch in one corner, and shelves full of books in another.

"That won't work here." I indicate the cell phone Bay's pulled from her pocket.

"I figured." She looks chagrined to be caught checking it, before she shoves it back into her pocket. "This is where we'll be staying for two whole nights?"

"Don't worry, my parents moved out when I went to college. They live off the grid now."

"This isn't off the grid?" She laughs.

"You'll have total privacy." I point to the door that leads into a second bedroom. "You have your own bed-room." I wince, wishing I'd thought this through better. When I asked her to come with me, all I could think about was being with her for the whole weekend. Now that we are here, the awkwardness of close proximity with someone I really want to sleep with seems more obvious.

"I kinda thought we'd be somewhere with more people—are you sure you won't get sick of me?" Her voice gets quieter as she continues to talk.

"I won't get sick of you," I say, "two days is hardly enough of you."

She squirms, but a light flashes in her eyes that gives me a wild hope she might spend more than just this weekend with me. I'm going to do everything I can for the next two days to keep her by my side. I need her to know this isn't just about sex for me, it isn't just physical, this is everything. She's mine completely, and this weekend, I will tell her everything. I'll explain that we are mates, and that we are meant to be together forever.

"You can unpack," I suggest, "I'm going to the river out back, to catch us dinner."

"Fishing? Can I come?" She has a wild grin. "I've never tried before!"

I love her enthusiasm for new things, but it's my turn to squirm at her request. I shake my head. "You might not appreciate the way I do it..."

"I wouldn't like the way you fish?" she asks with a laugh.

I grunt an affirmative, and she schools her features when it's clear that I'm uncomfortable.

"I'm sorry. I didn't mean to laugh. If you really don't want me there, then I'm happy to wait here, but now you've piqued my curiosity. I really do want to come with you, if you will let me. I don't think I'm going to be upset by it." She continues rambling through the strange tension in the air. "It's just really hard to imagine you doing something I wouldn't like."

She's going to see me act like a beast eventually, now is as good a time as any. I take a deep breath before gesturing at her bedroom door. "Change into something you don't mind getting wet, and meet me outside."

She hurries off with her luggage. I drop my own gear into the other bedroom, the one that my parents shared. Then, I head outside to wait for my mate. Taking her fishing may be a mistake. If anything is going to convince her we shouldn't be together, it will be letting her see my monstrous side. It's easy to ignore my inhuman qualities when I'm wearing a suit.

But when she joins me, I realize telling her how to dress may have been a far more dangerous mistake.

She walks out in blue yoga shorts that hug her luscious ass, a pink bikini top, and a sheer white bathing suit coverup, her full breasts threatening to spill out. This outfit is going to have me acting like a monster soon enough.

Fuck, what have I gotten myself into? How am I going to keep my hands off this woman this weekend?

"Something wrong?" she asks. "Should I change?" She looks down at the outfit, while I blatantly stare.

"No! No. You look great!"

She gives me an impish smile. The little minx knows exactly what she's doing. "Then let's go fishing!" she announces loudly and lets me lead her to the river.

18

PLEASE DO NOT RUN

BAILEY

I follow Sacha along a narrow dirt trail, through some muddy woods, and down a hill to something that could only generously be called a river. The water is narrow and shallow, but moving fast over uneven rocks, it's easily traversable by foot. The summer air is heavy with the cool spray of water. I give a small shiver, and for a moment, wish I'd dressed warmer, but the look that Sacha gave me when I revealed my bathing suit is worth being chilly for a little while. If I'm going to spend the entire weekend with him, I may as well soak up a little of his admiration. The sun filters through the branches of the cedar trees high above us; it's a truly perfect day.

Sacha really looks like he belongs here. He seems more relaxed, at ease in his own skin, happier. He rolls up the legs of his pants above his knee, revealing hairy but muscular legs. He pauses, giving me a long pointed look.

"Are you sure you are ready to see this?" He asks.

"What could you possibly do here that would make me upset?" I settle onto a large rock sitting on the riverbank. "Honestly, the suspense is killing me."

He gives a bemoaned sigh and then reaches over his head to his back, grips his shirt, and pulls it over his head in one smooth movement, revealing a broad muscular

chest. It's everything I imagined and still steals my breath for a moment. His hair thins out along his chest and stomach, displaying deep orange skin, and a stretch of rippling muscles that appear to have been sculpted by the finest personal trainers. He looks good enough to eat off of, certainly good enough to lick.

"Don't say I didn't warn you," Sacha interrupts my daydream, seeming to mistake my silence for trepidation.

"If I hate it that much, then I get half a million dollars!" I announce loudly over the sound of running water. "Let's get this over with! Catch me some dinner!"

He shrugs, but tosses me his shirt, the fabric still warm as I clutch it between my hungry fingers. He steps into the water, wading aimlessly through the rapids while staring at his feet. Eventually, he reaches a spot, which doesn't look any different than the others from my vantage point, but he finally seems satisfied with his position and he stops moving.

He stands completely still, watching the water rush between his legs.

"Did you just realize that you forgot your fishing rod?" I call to him.

He doesn't look up, but I do see a smile creep across his face.

And then one large hand shoots out, slapping into the water, and comes back up with a large fish wiggling in his grip.

I shout gleefully as he approaches.

"That's amazing!" I announce when he brings his catch over to me. "How do you do that?"

"You aren't—weirded out by it?" He shakes his head and drops the fish into the bucket he brought along.

"No, it's cool! I don't know anyone who can do any-thing like that!" I say with a laugh. "It's impressive."

"You don't think it's—monstrous?"

I shift in my seat. "Maybe? But, I think it's kind of hot."

Something in his smile changes as he looks at me. Water drips down his chest, begging for me to chase it with my tongue. I wait for him to tip in and kiss me, instead he turns back to the river and catches two more salmon to join the first. I get to enjoy the smooth and confident way that he moves, the way that his powerful muscles flex while he works. He smiles at me, all shiny white teeth, and runs his hand back across his damp chest.

"I want to try it," I announce as he drops the third fish into the bucket.

He gives me a questioning look. "I think we have enough. I should clean these and get dinner started."

"Show me how?" I ask, watching his face as I stand. I pull off my bathing suit coverup and relish the way his eyes drink in my chest and soft stomach.

He lets me use his powerful arm for support as I gingerly step into the moving water with him. He shows me how to keep my balance in the rushing water, points out the path of the fish, shows me how to shape my hand, and how to strike into the water as quickly as possible.

I do not resist the urge to lean back and press my body into the shell of his, letting his chest make contact with my exposed skin.

He points to a shimmering fish and gives me an encouraging nudge. I twist, trying to keep my ass at a flattering angle to Sacha as I move in the fish's path, only to immediately lose my footing on the slippery rocks.

I fall onto my butt in the shallow water.

Large hands circle my waist and effortlessly lift me, setting me back on my feet.

"Are you alright?" Sacha's face is full of concern.

"Fine, fine," I assure him, the only thing truly bruised is my dignity, "Just a little wet."

His face breaks into a grin. "Maybe you should leave the fishing to me?"

"Excuse me! That was my first time!" I exclaim. "I only have the opportunity to improve from here. Were you this good at fishing the first time that you tried it?"

"Well, I didn't fall on my ass..."

"You are an ass!" I announce, splashing a small amount of water in his direction.

"You are a beast!" He laughs, and I send another splash in his direction before he skirts his large arm across the surface of the water, creating a tidal wave that douses me. I screech and duck away, before running for the river bed with a laugh as he sends another large wave of water toward my back.

"Just try and get me on dry land!" I challenge, sticking my tongue out at him.

"Bay, do not run from me." He growls, the noise sending a little shiver down my spine. "You do not want me to chase you."

"I think I might." I laugh.

His eyes darken, the threat in his voice holds an exciting promise that has me gasping before I turn and dart up the path we followed to the river.

He lets out a roar. The noise that echoes through the trees makes my heart beat faster and sends a thrilling pulse straight to my pussy.

I laugh, but run a little faster, leaping off the little dirt trail and into the tree line.

Behind me, large feet crash through the undergrowth.

I duck behind a tree, putting my back to the trunk. I've stopped for less than a breath when a strong arm circles me, pulling me sideways and pressing my back against a wide flat chest. He heaves me off the ground so that my feet dangle uselessly in the air. His arms splay over my front, spreading heat across my body, one arm crosses my waist as the other creeps up my chest. Tilting my head back and up so large fingers can wrap gently around my neck, my hands grasp his hairy forearm and heavy breath tickles my ear.

"Fuck. You really are a beast, aren't you? Running away from me, like frightened little prey." His voice is almost pained.

He presses his nose to my hair, sucking in a long, deep breath before his lips press a light kiss to my hot skin. Desire shoots through my limbs. I'm at his mercy like this, completely trapped by his grip. My body shivers with need.

"You can't do that, my beast. I like seeing you run from me. I like it too much," He mutters against my skin. His grip squeezes me against his body, pressing my ass into a thick, hard rod that proves just how much he likes it. "Running makes me see you as prey, and there are only two things I do with prey."

"What's that?"

"Eat it, or fuck it."

His dark voice sends a pulse through my clit, and something like a whimper escapes my tightly pressed lips.

"That noise isn't helping. Run from me again, and I might not be able to stop myself. Do you understand, my beast? You treat me like a man, but I'm a monster, with urges and dark desires that you might not understand, and I don't know if I can control it."

His thumb traces back and forth across the sensitive column of my throat. I feel my pulse racing under his hand. He's terrifying, and strong, and wonderful.

"Okay," I give a shaky nod.

"I don't want to act like an animal," he growls, "but next time I catch you, the beast in me will have to fuck you against a tree until you are screaming for mercy. Please, do not run from me."

Hell. Hell, and shit, and fuck. That sounds too good.

"I won't run." I promise him, finally wetting my dry mouth. I feel like all the moisture in my body is pooling somewhere else.

"Good girl." His voice is serious as he slowly lets me slip down his body to the ground. "Now, let me take you home and make you dinner, like a gentleman would."

He takes a step away from me, and my whole back grows cold. My feet are frozen in place, contemplating his promise, but also his plea. I'm not sure I want him to be a gentleman, but I don't know if I am ready to tempt the monster inside him right now, not when he asked me not to. Sacha trudges back down the dirt trail back to the river, retrieving our clothing and our dinner. Without a word, he hands me my bathing suit cover-up, the bucket of fish in his other hand. He barely meets my eye as we walk back to the cabin. He seems embarrassed and ashamed, but every part of me feels highlighted. Alive with need.

"I need to change," I announce loudly when we step into the cabin. I race to my bedroom, locking the door behind me.

The ache between my legs reminds me that it's been a long time since I let anyone into my pants. I should just go back out there and fuck him, shouldn't I?

The fact that I want to so badly means it's a bad idea. I'm such a fool about men, males. He's not a man, he's a monster. He said as much himself. Even coming here with him was probably a mistake. A remote location with a male I barely know. A male with big warm hands and a big hard chest, and a big fat cock. My friends don't even know where exactly I am. He could do anything to me, and I might let him.

I lean my back to the door and shove my hand down the waistband of my wet shorts. Creeping my fingers beneath my underwear and press between my thighs, down toward the needy heat of my core. I stroking my fingers between my lips and across my clit. I'm already so wet. It's easy to indulge myself in a few fantasies of Sacha. Him bursting through my door, climbing on top of me, or taking me against the wall. Chasing me down the way he promised he would.

He's always making promises, but what if I ran out there right now? Ran past him. Would he chase me into the woods? Push me down into the dirt? Shove his cock into me?

I grab a breast, rolling a nipple between two fingers, and bite back a groan. Wishing it was his hand on me, his mouth, his cock pleasuring me, using me for his own desires. I slip another finger inside myself and have to drop my breast and shove my knuckle into my mouth to stop a groan from escaping. I am sure that he would hear it, hear me. It only makes me want him more. The idea of him on the other side of the door only makes me clench around my fingers tighter. I whisper his name as I come.

19

THE ONLY THING I DON'T HAVE IS HER

SACHA

Fuck. What have I done? What did I almost do? Chasing her down, attacking her in the woods, holding her captive against me. I can't believe I lost control that way. I couldn't stop myself until I felt her soft wiggling body in my arms, completely at my mercy.

Behavior like that is going to scare her off. I have to be able to control myself if I'm going to convince her to stay with me.

Still, I loved every second of it, the way she felt trapped against me, the way my fingers dug into her flesh, the way her heart raced, the way fear and adrenaline tinted her smell. I loved that she ran from me, the way she whimpered like a little animal, the way it made me want to claim her.

If I let those primal instincts take over, I'll scare her off. I'm not a human—I'm a monster.

I barely speak to her on our walk back to the cabin and, the second we step inside, Bailey disappears into her room. Almost like she can't stand to be near me for another moment. I don't blame her. I could kick myself for acting like that. It doesn't matter how long I've spent

115

living with the humans, or how many fancy suits I buy, none of it squashes my monstrous instincts.

Pacing the main room of the cabin, I try to expend some of my extra energy, but in the cramped space, there's only a couple steps for my bare feet to travel. I need her so badly. My cock went hard the instant she ran away from me, and it's still a solid rod in my pants. I just need to release some of this pressure, but it's difficult when she's so close and smells so good. The whole cabin is permeated with her scent now.

She's like a skittish little animal fleeing me, and as enticing as I find that, I need to let her come to me. I cannot indulge in my desire to chase her through the woods, throw her down to the ground, and fuck her. She thinks this relationship is just about sex, but if I want to keep her forever, then I need her to know I am serious about her.

I have the money, the status, and the strength. The only thing I don't have is her.

She is meant to be my mate, I can feel it. I have never wanted a woman the way that I want her, and the more time that we spend together, the more I know that the mating bond is right. We are meant for each other.

From my past experiences with humans, I know so much of me is terrifying. I'm all muscles, with sharp teeth, too much hair, and instincts that are untenable to their kind. If my mate had been another Bigfoot, I could have avoided this, but I'm destined to be with a human. This beautiful soft woman who is hiding from me while I stew in regret for attacking her. My feet find a path to her bedroom door, even as I fight the urge to knock and apologize for my behavior. I should give her space, let her have time alone until she's ready to come out and speak with me.

Then, her scent hits me. Her arousal is so thick that it seeps through the door of her bedroom and assaults my senses. I lean against the smooth surface of the door before I even realize what I'm doing.

My body trying to get closer to the scent of her, the heady smell of her arousal, without any intention from my brain. I draw in a deep breath to soak up more of her smell. River water drips from my still-wet legs onto the wood floor. I wish there was no door here. I could just be with her, in her arms, between her legs, coating myself with her scent.

My dick is hard in my pants just remembering how soft she is, how she felt wrapped in my arms, how she squirmed and whimpered and ran from me, the way her pulse raced beneath my grip, the way her plump ass cushioned my erection. I want her beneath me, coming apart on my cock. Looking me in the eye and screaming my name as she comes.

I pull down my pants, wrap my fist around my erection, and tug; wishing that it was my mate's touch on me. Instead of my own punishing grip, it should be her hand, her mouth, her pussy.

I press my ear to the door, wanting nothing more than to tear it from its hinges to be near her. My pumps speed up when, on the other side of the wood, she makes a soft sound. In that noise I think I hear my name, that pushes me over the edge. I spill my cum onto my own stomach.

Fuck. I want her. I cannot keep acting like an animal in front of her. She will never stay with me if I do. I race to clean myself up before she can see me in this ridiculous state. I change, putting myself back together, into a gentleman, someone a human wouldn't be ashamed to be with, and when I walk out of my bedroom, hair combed and outfit nicely in place, I start making dinner.

20

HOT PASTRAMI

BAILEY

When I emerge from my bedroom in a dry outfit and a clean pair of underwear, Sacha already has dinner cooking on the stove. His back stays to me, even though I'm sure he heard me walk into the room.

"It smells wonderful," I announce.

"Thank you." He glances over his shoulder with a polite nod before turning back to the pan grilling on a small gas stove.

I double check my appearance for any evidence that I was rubbing one out to him a few minutes ago, but I think I'm safe. There's nothing suspicious about my outfit. Sweatpants and a baggy t-shirt, covering my least sexy sports bra and a gross pair of underwear. All of it was carefully selected for being far less provocative than my previous outfit. The flirty swimsuit almost got me in trouble.

He's in different clothes too. Dressed up rather than down, in a pair of pressed slacks, a button down shirt, and a blazer.

"Should I change?" I ask, feeling self conscious.

"No," he doesn't even turn around when he says it. "You look perfect."

His curt tone surprises me. "Can I help with anything?"

"The silverware is in the drawer here." He nods to one of the two drawers in the small kitchen.

I step toward it, and he jerks out of my way like I'm made out of hot coals.

So much for pretending nothing happened.

I set the small table with plates and cutlery. Then, with a loss for conversation, I sit quietly in one of the Bigfoot-sized chairs, to wait for him to finish cooking. My toes barely graze the ground. I swing my feet idly, wondering if I should apologize for everything that happened earlier. I knew he'd get sick of me eventually, but I didn't think it would be this quickly, and not because of a silly sexy game of chase through the woods.

Dinner turns out to be grilled salmon and kale salad. It's the most beautiful home cooking I've seen in a long time. He's clearly familiar with the kitchen.

"I know it's not much," He sets two perfectly plated meals on the table.

"Not much?!" I exclaim. "This looks fantastic." I slice off a bite with my fork and slip it into my mouth, the fish is grilled to perfection, it practically melts on my tongue. "My god, this is fucking amazing!"

His face flicks into a small smile before it drops again. I hate that everything feels different. We were having such a nice time. I felt like I was really getting to know him.

"Sorry," I say.

"Please, Ms. Thorn, don't apologize for enjoying yourself."

"Oh." I set down my utensils.

"Something wrong?"

"Are we back to Ms. Thorn?"

He drops his gaze, pushing his food around his plate with his fork. "I'm very sorry about losing control earlier. I shouldn't have let my baser instincts get the better of me. It wasn't the right way to treat you—to treat a human." His grip around his silverware tightens, while his eyes remain glued to his plate.

"Who told you that?"

He finally looks up. "I know Bigfoots have different relationship habits than humans."

"Yeah? So?" I ask.

He leans away from the table. "Human women don't enjoy being chased through the woods."

"We don't?" I ask. "This is news to me."

His eyebrow raises. "You don't need to pretend for me. I want you to be comfortable. The humans I've dated in the past—"

"If you want me to be comfortable, then you shouldn't bring up women that you'd dated in the past," I grumble.

He swallows hard, but continues anyway. "They didn't appreciate my more monstrous ways."

"Ahh... I see. Is that why you are wearing the—" I gesture to his outfit.

"It makes me feel more human. I thought you liked the way I look in a suit?"

"I do like the way you look in a suit. I like the way that you look in most things." I shake my head, shocked I'm admitting these things out loud. Even if we aren't going to stay together, it still feels important to get it off my chest. I don't want him to think he did something wrong. "I don't mind if you don't act human. You aren't human. I want—shit." My brain jumbles up all my thoughts the way it always does when I just need to get words out. "You know. I Googled you, after you offered me this dating deal—thing. I looked you up online, and I saw pictures of you with the other women that you've dated. They didn't exactly look like me."

"I've dated human women before."

"They were human women, but they were all—" I inhale, knowing that I'm about to open a can of worms that I might not be prepared for, "they were all skinny. With perky little breasts and low BMIs. Beautiful women, certainly. It's fine, of course. They all had good jobs, money, and status." The words fall out of me in a rush.

"What does that have to do with anything?" He scowls.

"If I were to follow that thought to its natural conclusion, I'd assume that you don't find me attractive." I adjust myself in my seat, sitting up straighter. "I'm comfortable with my body most of the time, but why would you want to date me when you usually date women who are much thinner and richer than me?"

His fist closes tightly around his fork. "Beast, you are perfect. I wouldn't change a single thing about you or your body."

"Wouldn't you?"

"Of course not. I like you exactly the way you are. I think you are perfect. Just because of something you saw in my past, you shouldn't assume—" he pauses, "I see."

"You shouldn't make assumptions about what people want. You don't want me to change, and I don't need you to change." I point at him with my fork. "And fuck those women for making you feel like you couldn't be yourself around them. We will both be ourselves, in our own skin. I will let you know when you have made me uncomfortable."

There is finally something almost like a smile creeping across his lips.

"Would you like to ask me anything about today?" I point to myself. "Like if I enjoyed myself?"

"Did you enjoy yourself today?" he asks.

"I had a lot of fun. A lot. I learned how to fish with my hands, that river rocks can be very slippery, and that I should not run away from a Bigfoot unless I am ready to deal with the consequences."

He freezes. "Bailey, I will never—"

"And, when I am ready to deal with the consequences, believe me, I will let you know," I say quickly before he can finish. It's a terrifying thing to promise. It may be a bad idea, but my brain is determined to try it before I leave him.

His face relaxes a little. "Thank you, my beast."

There is a long moment of quiet, which is broken by the scrape of his chair legs across the floor as he stands before removing his suit jacket, folding it neatly, and draping it over the back of a chair. The little signal of trust makes my heart flutter.

Then he unbuttons his shirt enough for some of his copious chest hair to peek out, reminding me of the unfettered view I was presented earlier today, and that makes my coochie flutter.

"Maybe you'll get another chance to teach me to fish?" I suggest.

"I would enjoy seeing you wet again." He gives me a very small, very promising, smirk.

"That's probably doable." I bite my lip, and he looks at me with his big brown eyes that make the room feel lighter. "Dinner was fantastic. Maybe you could teach me how to cook as well."

"I cooked a lot of meals when we were just a start-up without any money for food. A lot of that was cheap ramen, or beans and rice, but I'm glad the skills I acquired

can finally impress someone." He starts clearing the empty dishes from the table.

I lean back in my chair, watching Sacha carefully roll up his sleeves and starts washing dishes. The night is young, I'm not tired, and I want to spend more time with him. "I only wish that, maybe, we had something for dessert."

"Check in the cupboard over there." Sacha nods to a cabinet.

I open it to find a grocery bag with chocolate bars, a box of graham crackers, and a bag of marshmallows.

"Oh, shit. Are you serious? S'mores!" I cannot keep from grinning.

"I thought we could roast the marshmallows over the fire? Outside?"

"Hell yes, we can! You managed to think of everything! Are you fucking perfect, or what?"

"Maybe I'm perfect for you?" He teases me again with one of those beautiful smiles.

He's very nearly perfect. Except that he's my boss, and he is technically bribing me to be here. Except that I'm going to break up with him when we get back to the city. Except that I have to leave him before he gets a chance to get tired of me, I just can't give another person a chance to drop me from their life.

21

LET ME CLEAN YOU OFF

BAILEY

Sacha builds a fire in the pit in front of the cabin. It's surrounded by hand-carved benches, some of the seats worn smooth from years of use. The evening is waning, but this time of summer, the sun doesn't properly set until late after dinner. Crickets chirp angrily at us from the growing darkness while Sacha tosses another piece of wood onto the fire.

I settle into one of the benches, nearly dwarfed by the Bigfoot-sized furniture, and enjoy the crackle of the wood. Sacha produces two metal-pronged sticks, perfect for roasting marshmallows, before he sits on the other end of the bench. As the night moves on, we find excuses to move closer and closer together until his leg is flush with mine. We stuff our faces with chocolate and marshmallows smushed between crunchy graham crackers. His arm finds its way around my shoulder as we watch the beautiful sky, stars twinkling into view that are never this visible in the crowded city.

"There," Sacha takes the opportunity to lean further into my space and points to a constellation, "is the Big Dipper."

I reach up, wrapping my hand around his, and guide it across the visible sky. "Scorpio." I trace the outline of the constellation. "Sagittarius," I add with a smile.

He catches my hand in his with a small laugh. "Alright, show off, I never learned that many of them."

"I did astrology readings for a while in college." I stroke my thumb along his knuckles, my hands dwarfed by his large fingers. "Nothing serious, just a little cash on the side. I couldn't quite convince myself to really believe in it, and then giving readings felt like lying."

"I am continually impressed by you, Beast."

When I turn to him, he's staring at me intensely—too intensely for me to keep making eye contact. I move my eyes back to the sky with a shrug. "You are the impressive one. I've never built a company from scratch. I've barely held a single job for six months."

Sacha shakes his head. "You've chased your heart through so many phases and adventures. I've been doing the same tired thing for years on end."

"Yeah, and you have the money and status to show for your efforts."

"Hmph," he snorts, "you are brave. Always willing to try something new, rather than stay in the same safe place."

I swallow hard. "Hardly brave. I don't have to face that I'm bad at things if I'm always moving on to a new challenge. You can't get rejected if you quit first."

He nudges my shoulder, and when I look at him, he swipes a finger of melted chocolate over my cheek.

"Hey!" I yelp.

"You could do anything if you really set your mind to it. You are brave, and talented, and smart."

"And dirty," I mutter, reach a hand up to swipe at my cheek.

126

"Sorry about that." He catches my hand before it reaches my cheek and gives a devilish grin. "Let me clean you off."

He drops my hand to cup my face in one large hand, my breath catches as he leans in close and swipes his lips across my skin, licking my face clean. A warm chuckle sends his hot breath glancing against my cheek.

"There, my beautiful beast is all clean."

I start to laugh, but he leans forward, catches my giggle with his mouth, and the world seems far from funny. He presses kisses to me, soft and generous, until my lips are parting and his tongue is dipping into my mouth, exploring me. He holds back even as I push forward against his strong, broad body, kneading his chest with my hands until I am almost groaning into his mouth. A frustrating heat builds in my core. His touch remains reserved, even though I can feel the urgency growing in his pants.

"Sacha, I'm on the pill. We can—If you want to—" My whispered words fumble to a stop. "I've been tested."

There is the briefest of hesitations from him.

"Bailey," his hand traces up my thigh, "we don't need to have sex tonight."

My brain nearly implodes at his words. Is he really turning me down? Again? Here? "Seriously?"

"I want to enjoy every part of you, but I want you to know you are fully in control here." His voice is dark and serious.

"I'm not sure I want to be in control." I croak out the words before thinking about them.

"I need you to feel safe with me." One of his hands slips up my ribcage, his thumb grazing softly along the side of my breast. "I need you to know that I can control myself."

"I do. I feel very safe with you, Sacha, even here in the middle of the woods, with no cell service. I've never known someone with as much self-control as you." I feel so safe that I am growing more and more certain that am going to get my heart broken. I press my thigh into the palm he rests there. He groans, his large hand tightening around my leg. I would probably do anything to get him to keep touching me right now. "Fuck it. Just tell me, what are you stopping yourself from doing?"

"Beast, I need to taste you." He growls, and my entire crotch melts into a pool.

"Oh, fuck. Yes, please," I say gratefully, and his mouth falls onto me again as his hand creeps up under my shirt to caress across my breasts.

His fingers edge along my sports bra, the one that I wear when I don't care if I have uni-boob, the one I wore to try and deter myself from allowing this exact situation. It isn't cute, but Sacha is completely undeterred, tugging fabric in various directions until my chest is free. Tossing first my shirt and then the bra to the ground. His eyes fall on me in the firelight. It can be difficult to navigate the world as a plus-sized woman, but I've worked on my self image enough that I am confident in my body.

Still, I've never felt sexier than now, with his gaze drinking me in. His hands move reverentially across my round stomach. He releasing a growl before his mouth can find my breast, wrapping his tongue around my nipple and toying with me until I am whimpering beneath him.

His hand rests at my waist, fingers dipping slightly into the elastic waistband of my sweats. This outfit is absolutely terrible. I cannot believe it is going to get me laid.

"No, wait, wait—" I say. He freezes instantly, his hands easing their grip on my thighs, and his eyes flying to mine.

"Too fast? Too much?" He's breathing hard, the firelight catching him in wild dancing shadows, and I've never seen anything more attractive.

"I haven't—cleaned up down there."

One of his eyebrows raises.

"I didn't think we'd be doing this. I didn't shave." I clarify before burying my face in my hands so I can't see him.

Sacha chuckles low, and pulls my hands from my eyes. "Beast, do you think that I am bothered by a little hair?"

"Probably not." I squirm under him.

His hand meets my breast again. He kisses me long and hard until I am moaning against his lips, and then his fingers slowly find the waistband of my pants again, dipping just under the fabric but not moving any further.

I give him an enthusiastic nod this time, too turned on to be deterred by any of the road blocks I put in place to prevent this. No amount of body hair or bad underwear is going to keep me from knowing what this male's tongue feels like. He jerks down my pants, his hands stroking up and down my bare thighs as he looks me over, tracing every curve of my body with his eyes and his fingers.

"You look delectable, I bet you are delicious," he murmurs words of praise. "Open your legs for me, Beautiful."

It's half a question and half a command, I let my thighs fall apart, letting the night air caress my wet pussy.

"Good girl." He presses a kiss to the inside of each knee, then slowly moves his lips down the inside of my thigh until his mouth finally meets the neediest part of me with voracious enthusiasm. Tongue and suction meet me until I am a panting, yelping mess underneath him, and then he presses a finger deep inside me. It curls and strokes, until he hits the perfect spot that shoots sparks through my limbs and I cry out.

"Right there. Right there! Sacha! Just like that!" My fingers dig into his shoulders, and bless him, he actually stays right there.

His finger repeating the curl, and his tongue lashing in the same way, until the walls of my pussy clench around him so tightly that lights twinkle behind my eyelids, mimicking the ones in the sky. My body surges forward, nearly folding in on itself. Still, his mouth stays right where it is, right where I need it, as he catches the aftershocks, the waves that ripple across me again, and again, and again until I have to pull him away from my sensitive clit.

Panting and overstimulated, I tug his face up to mine and kiss him. Hungry and cloudy-headed. I need more of him, more of him pressed against me. His face and beard are wet with my fluids. We taste so sweet together.

"Thank you, thank you, thank you," I mutter as I become aware of the wood underneath my naked body, and the way the fire heats half of me while the night air cools my skin on the other side. "You are, really, really, very good at that."

His hands rest beside my head, his arms trembling, and when I glance down, his dick pitches an impressive tent under his trousers, with a small wet spot just at the tip that shows just how excited he really is.

"Sacha. Do you—want me to?" I can barely catch my breath. The outline of his dick has another wave of desire passing over me. I move my hand down his chest, toward his belt buckle. He catches my hand in his.

"No—no—tonight is for—" He pulls back from me, his body quivering. "Let me show you I have control. Let me do this for you tonight."

"That doesn't seem fair at all." My words are lost in the night air as he kisses me again, his hand finding my nipple, then his lips, then his mouth and tongue. He repeats the same order between my thighs until I am screaming his name over and over. I keep waiting for him to push for more, to suggest another step, to take us to the next level, instead it's just me, again and again, until I'm no longer begging him to continue, and just asking him to stop.

"Please, Sacha. It has to be your turn now," I murmur as he tucks me against his chest. "You've done so much for me."

"Shush, my beast. There's time for that later." He presses a kiss to my forehead.

I know he's wrong. There won't be time later. We have right now, this weekend, and that's all, but my eyelids are so heavy that when I blink, I'm not sure how much time has passed. I'm partially aware of his large arms lifting me, carrying me inside, arranging me gently on the large soft bed and covering me with a blanket. I'm half aware of the chilly emptiness that remains as he leaves. A small part of me protests that he's leaving, but that part doesn't manage to overpower my eyelids as they close.

22

WOULDN'T DEMEAN YOUR TALENT

BAILEY

I wake up alone, which I expected. The bed is enormous and extra long, presumably to accommodate a Bigfoot body. The room is so small it's practically one big bed. It's actually a very cozy feeling, and even though I usually sleep alone and relish my space, I feel a twinge of loneliness when I spread my arms wide and find nothing but cool sheets.

I roll to my feet and throw an easy summer dress over my body. I fell asleep naked. Sacha left my clothes from the night before folded neatly at the foot of my bed. Even my ratty old sports bra. I hope he doesn't think all of my underwear is that unattractive. I slip on a cute lacy pair just in case.

The morning sun is just blooming through the bedroom's small window. I wonder if Sacha has anything planned for the day. I creep into the main room of the cabin, only to find it empty. A French press full of coffee sits steaming beside the stove, and Sacha's bedroom door is wide open, showing that the cabin is vacant. I'm glad that he let me sleep in, but a flair of terror blooms through me that maybe he's abandoned me here.

133

It's ridiculous, I know it is. It's stupid to be scared. Still, I have to take a deep breath to quash my fear as I shakily pour myself a mug of coffee.

Doing so, I spot the note next to the carafe.

Gone swimming. See you soon.
xoxo, Sacha

The words bring me a modicum of reassurance. He's coming back. I knew he would. Of course he is. Of course he is.

I breathe my anxiety slowly out my mouth as I step onto the front porch with my cup of coffee. Being alone gives me a chance to enjoy the solitude the cabin provides. The sun has mostly risen, but there are still long shadows this deep in the woods. Nearly everything is cast in a level of darkness, but soon summer will be hot and heavy outside. I pad barefoot across the soft grass, slowly circling the cabin, admiring the small details added by his family over the years. The air is still and easy, with the heavy scent of pine. I've never been much for wilderness, but I'm starting to understand the attraction of seclusion. It's so peaceful here—so peaceful I don't notice at first when Sacha walks into view.

His back is to me, and he doesn't seem to know I'm there. His fur is dripping wet from the river, the only thing he's wearing is a towel wrapped loosely around his waist. Another glorious reason to enjoy being secluded. A handsome Bigfoot can walk around half-naked.

He looks good.

Really. Really. Good.

I take a moment to enjoy the sight. His hair is still wet from the river. It's plastered to his body, covering his broad shoulders and back, but thins out across his chest and stomach, rivulets of water run down his chest into those v-shaped muscles of his adonis belt that funnel right to the edge of the towel draped across his hips.

It brings back pleasant memories of the night before—his fingers, mouth, and tongue. The mindless, uncountable orgasms that rocked me. I have to fuck him before we leave. Maybe I could even get him to chase me later.

I should have dragged him into my bed last night. I should have fucked him in the woods when he offered. When am I going to get a chance like this again? A super hot, super rich guy who claims he wants to be with me? I can just let him have me, can't I? For a little while, at least? The money he pays me will make up for whatever emotional damage he causes.

Before I can utter a breath, he drops the towel, his body fully on display now, revealing a long thick cock dangling between his legs, reaching nearly halfway down his thigh. He lifts his long arms above his head in a laborious stretch, still seemingly ignorant of my presence. His mouth opens large to releases a wide yawning roar that shakes the trees.

Shit. I should say something. I should look away. I definitely shouldn't let my gaze linger on the shadow his dick casts on his thigh.

His skin twitches, and he shakes like a dog. His whole body shimmies, water sprays in every direction, and his cock flops in the air, slapping against each of his tree trunk thighs. It catches me off guard, and I squeak as a drop of water hits me.

His head whips around.

"Sorry!" I slap my hands over my eyes. "I didn't mean to watch! I mean—I didn't mean to see everything! Sorry!"

"Bay!" He says some more words after that, but the noise is lost in chaos as I repeatedly spout an apology.

"Sorry, sorry, sorry." I continue as I turn and run for the front door of the cabin.

"Bay! Do not run!" he bellows after me.

I'm too lost in embarrassment to comprehend. I race around the corner of the house, bound up the steps of the front porch, before I realize what I am doing. I try to stop myself, but I as I stumble to a halt, my bare foot catches on the front door jam. I tumble to my knees inside the cabin with a yelp.

And then he's on top of me. His heavy weight pins me easily to the floor.

"I told you not to run," he growls into my ear. His rough hands meet my waist, and he effortlessly lifts me, flipping me onto my back. He pins my hands above my head, both of my wrists held in one large, capable hand. He spreads my thighs with the press of his knee as he lowers himself over me. My brain is flooded, half with fear and half with desire. He's strong and big, and I'm totally at his mercy.

"Sacha!" It's not a protest. He's still completely naked. I can feel how aroused he is. His erection is pressed against me so close and hard that, if I wasn't wearing underwear, he'd be inside me right now. My brain is screaming for him to pull them to the side and shove his cock into me, but fortunately, my mouth stays closed.

He doesn't move for what feels like an eternity, but is truthfully only a few ragged breaths. There's a terrifying, beautiful, thrilling darkness in his eyes.

He's panting, like the effort of not taking me here on the bare floor of the cabin is too much exertion for him. "Fuck. I'm sorry, Beast." His voice is a raspy growl that only makes my pussy wetter.

"It's okay," I whisper, scared to say more in case I demand that he fucks me.

He leans back, releasing my wrists to cover his face with his hands. The unignorable tension on my underwear eases. "I'm so sorry, Bailey. Are you alright?"

"I'm fine." I reassure him. I'm better than fine, I'm burning for him right now.

But he keeps his face hidden in a way that has me worried. In an effort to console him, I reach up to stroke a hand across his cheek and dig my fingers into his beard.

"I'm so sorry." He pulls away from my touch and leaps to his feet, pulling a blanket from the couch to hide his erection. I'm a little sad not to get a better look at it, but even more upset that he doesn't want me touching him. "This is how Bigfoots work. We hunt to eat, and we hunt to mate. I didn't mean to—I wasn't thinking."

"It's okay. You warned me. I'm sorry, I shouldn't have—"

"No." He cuts me off loudly. "Do not apologize. This is my fault. I should be in better control. You shouldn't be scared I'm going to lose it like this."

I sit up, straightening my clothes. "You didn't hurt me. I know you wouldn't hurt me." I feel the truth of the words deep in my gut as I say them. "I wasn't scared. Well—I guess I was a little scared, but way more turned on than scared."

His expression changes to something tormented, and his hand wipes across his face, like he's trying to clear the emotion.

"I know you can control yourself." I pull myself into a kneeling position in front of him. "It's you that doesn't trust yourself." I run a hand up his hairy leg.

"Bailey," his voice is pained.

"You have control, Sacha," I say. "I can prove it to you. Sit down, I'll show you."

"Bailey," he repeats, but his eyes finally meet mine, looking down from his impressive height. He holds the blanket tight in one hand as the other strokes tenderly through my hair.

"Sit," I say again, digging my fingers into the thick hair of his leg. I push him gently toward the couch. "Sit down, and let me see what I do to you."

23

GUYS WITH BIG FEET

BAILEY

I tug at the blanket that he holds. Sacha's grip loosens, letting me pull it to the side to reveal his erection. It stands almost painfully at attention. He sinks slowly to the couch, and I position myself between his knees.

My eyes lock on the largest cock I have ever seen.

"I guess, it's true what they say about guys with big feet." I breathe in admiration.

He gives a small groan and starts to pull away from me, but when I press a cheek against the inside of his leg, he settles and letting me examine him.

It's curved up a little, and the color is a slightly darker orange than the rest of his skin. It looks like a human dick, for the most part. Except that he's huge—larger than any I've ever seen before. It might be too big. It might be more than I could possibly take. My pussy clenches just thinking about it. I reach my hand out and gently trace a finger across the ballsack and up the vein on the underside of his shaft; he shudders and groans under my touch.

"What's this?" My hand strokes across the thick knob—almost the size of my fist— at the base of his cock, both a threat and a promise.

"A knot—" he murmurs, "it's for mating, a mating bond—it locks us together—fuck—Beast." His words break off into a groan as my hand traces him. His fists clench into the couch cushion instead of touching me. "You don't need to—fuck." His voice cuts out completely when I lick him, pressing my tongue against his hairy sack.

"How about," I let my breath hit his bare skin, "for right now, I am the boss. And I get to do whatever I want?"

He gives a low guttural groan that can only be a mangled agreement.

I grip a hand around him, exploring the shape of his hot length. He's so thick that my fingers don't even meet.

"I'm in charge," I repeat, my grin growing as I enjoy the way that sounds.

"Whatever you want," he croaks.

"What if I just teased you? Got your cock wet and walked away?"

He groans again, throwing his head back against the couch. "Whatever you want." His voice is more pained this time. "You're in control."

I let go of him and climb to my feet. I consider, for a moment, abandoning him there. Just letting him be hard, and hungry, and full. A very small part of me relishes the idea of leaving him like this.

But a much larger part of me wants to fuck him.

I really want to feel that thick cock inside me. There's something irresistible about him. His big, hairy body calls to me, and after the way he treated me last night, the way that he makes me feel tended to and cared for, I know this will feel good.

"You know what? This is perfect," I decide out loud, "I always have an easier time coming on top."

I meet his gaze, and his eyes widen. He gives me an eager nod, somehow knowing not to say anything.

I pull my dress up enough to slip a thigh onto either side of his thick legs, and slowly inch myself forward until I feel the thick shaft pressing against that spot it rested before, the barrier of my underwear keeping us apart. Fuck. He's big.

I roll my hips, dragging my body across him, the hot friction spark across my clit until it pulls a sound from my throat. Even with a layer of fabric between us, I could probably come just from this, just rubbing along him, teasing that burning hot length that nestles so nicely against me.

I love having him beneath me, with his head rolled back and his eyes pressed shut. He's huge, quivering, and completely at my mercy.

"Beast," he groans again. His large hands rest on my hips, smoothing up my thighs to skate beneath my dress and caress my naked skin. Not urging me to move, just stroking, worshiping. Lighting little fires across my excited body. Tracing paths along my body like all he wants to do is touch me.

I place my hands on his bare chest, using him to support my weight as I reach down, move my underwear to one side, and slide forward until I feel his needy tip slip into place, notching against the wet part of me that is so hungry for him. Fuck. Fuck. Fuck. I want him so badly.

His eyes fly open, dark brown irises devouring me, deep enough that I could get lost in them. His breathing is ragged, although I've barely moved. His hands are still stroking me, caressing, and petting, like he knows exactly how to light up every nerve in my skin. My body clenches, needing more of him, demanding something to clamp around. I need something inside me.

I dig my fingers into his chest hair.

"Beast," is all that he says, but somehow I feel the meaning behind the word. If we do this, I'm going to be

lost to him for sure, I'm not going to do the smart thing and take his money and walk away. I'm going to stay and let everything get messy and hot and sexy. I'm going to be stupid the way that I always am. I'm going to fall for the guy that I know I shouldn't fall for.

My thighs are trembling now. I sink an inch until his head is penetrating me. I gasp, and his fingers press deep into my thighs. Both of us are breathing hard now. I can feel wetness dripping out of me and down his length. How can I need him so badly? How is just the sight of him, the smell of him, this intoxicating?

I pull back up slowly, feeling the pop as he leaves me. The empty space in my body that needs him protests. He gasps beneath me, his hands going rigid against my thighs.

Then, with a deep resigned groan, I lower myself onto him again. Relishing the slow and aching stretch as I push myself further, and further, feeling the burn of him, the pressure of his size, the hot heat of his thickness. I bury my face into his neck, the musk caught in his fur sears my throat and catches the deep moan I release, as he fills every part of me. His hands are moving again, gently stroking and petting as he coos my name and whispers praises to me.

"Bailey. So good. My Beast. My mate. My good mate. My everything." I don't even know if he is saying full sentences. I'm too focused on the stretch of him, the fullness, and the tightness. The things that should be too much, but seems to fill me perfectly. Down and down, until I feel the threatening girth of his knot.

Fuck. I'm at my limit.

"I don't know if I can take it," I say against his neck.

"Don't, precious Beast. Not now. We have time for that later." He's whispering soothing words into my ear in his deep voice. It should be calming me down, but the sound only makes my pussy tighten around him.

Fuck. This isn't what this was supposed to be. This was supposed to be an easy orgasm, a quick couch fuck with all my clothes still on. Not this full body invasion, a complete overwhelming of my senses. I hear a soft whine come from my own throat as his hands keep moving across me, stroking along my thighs.

I rock against him, the pressure of my clit against his knot sends a fever through my body. The fullness of him quivering inside me, hitting every point, sends sparks all the way to the base of my skull. I grind against him slowly, letting the gentle pressure build and build. His hands, his cock, and his words apply themselves in tandem, until I am overwhelmed, and I tumble into ecstasy, my pussy clenching and milking him. A lightness rolls through my limbs that is so intense and lasts so long that I feel like I'm torn in two. I'm not sure if it is one long orgasm, or several, coming shockingly close together. He strokes my thighs, continuing to whisper deep, passionate words against my ear.

"Need—use me—Beast—Bailey—sweetness—mine."

The heat swirls through my body, tightening and loosening every muscle, until I can only collapse against him with a breathy sigh, whispering his name into his neck.

His fingers flex against my hips, digging into my flesh and asking, wordlessly, for permission.

"Sacha, do it," is all I can say.

He rewards me with a growl in my ear. His hands wrap around me, pressing me tight to his chest, one hand digging into my hair. He lifts my hips slightly, and then thrusts up with shocking power, pushing deep and hard against me, once, twice, three times before his mouth releases a loud howl as I feel him tighten and release inside me, shuddering and filling me with his seed, his mark, his cum, fuller than I thought I could ever be. His whole body spasms around mine, clenching and clinging to me. He holds to me against him, tugging my face into his neck.

He's hissing more words into my ear. Nonsense and platitudes, repeating 'mine' over and over, like I am a toy on a school yard to be claimed.

Then, he presses a gentle kiss to my forehead like the night before when he put me to bed. The barest brush of his lips reminds me that we haven't even kissed since we tumbled into the cabin. We managed this intensity, this raw passion, with my clothes on and barely any foreplay.

I've been thoroughly fucked, and I'm also completely screwed.

24

BEDROOM. RIGHT NOW

BAILEY

"Are you alright?" Sacha asks once the world has settled. He's maneuvered us on the couch so that he is lying on his back with me resting against his chest. I'd briefly tried to leave the room, but easily gave in when his hands pulled me close.

"I'm fine," I say. It's almost a lie. I feel like my entire world has been shattered. I was planning to walk away from this male. I told him this was our only weekend together, but I can already feel that I've changed everything with a little bit of sex. I focus on the rise of his breathing as it lifts me, and the sinking when he breathes back out, like his body is catching me as I fall. His hand strokes gently along my spine, comforting and warm.

"You know, those other women you saw photos of—" he begins.

"Do we really need to talk about them right now?" I ask with a long sigh.

"They never came here. With me. I've never invited anyone to my family's cabin before." He pauses while the words soak in, extra weight in the heavy silence. "You are special, Bailey Thorn."

"You keep saying that." I thread my hands through his chest hair, enjoying the hard muscle of his chest.

"Because I mean it," he says, "I have cherished every moment we've spent together."

My chest tightens when he talks like this. I want to believe him, to accept what he's offering me, but I might be too damaged to have everything I want. My hands find the side of his face, and I tilt his head, moving it so I can reach his mouth for a kiss. He makes a noise almost like a purr and tugs me up his body so he can press his lips more firmly to mine.

"Even though I've only had you for a little while," he says, "our time together has been perfect.."

"Only the weekend." I repeat the statement mostly to myself. I'm starting to feel like this relationship could be more than I originally thought, that maybe he actually means it when he said he wanted more than sex.

He kisses me again with that gentle heat that makes it easy to melt into him while his hands trace idle patterns up my back, gentle and slow. It makes me want to curl into him forever. He toys with the straps of my dress tugging, them to the sides until more of me is exposed, and then pulls me further up his body so that he can press his face into my bare breasts.

I laugh in protest, but it becomes a gasp as his warm mouth finds my nipple.

"Bailey, I need to tell you something, something about me—about us—" His speech is nervous and broken as his hand traces up my thigh, sneaking up to tease across the underwear I am still wearing.

"Now?" I ask.

"It has to be now, if you are only going to give me the weekend." His hands don't stop moving, his fingers find the curve of my ass and dig into my flesh just enough to spark a little pain to compliment the pleasure.

I moan, and his whole body stiffens.

"Did you hear that?" he whispers.

I shake my head but go still, listening. I'm beginning to realize most of my senses don't compare to his.

"Shit." He sits up suddenly, dislodging me from my wonderful resting spot.

Sacha maneuvers me easily, setting me on the couch beside him before leaping to his feet and, still fully nude, hurrying from the cabin.

I only have a moment to wonder where he's gone before he reappears in the doorway with a wide, terrified look in his eyes, his gaze sweeps over my frame.

"Is something wrong?" I ask.

"Bailey, go to the bedroom. Right now." Sacha's voice is quiet but urgent.

"What's happening?" I don't bother to correct the straps of my dress he dislodged earlier. He doesn't wait another second. He crosses the small room in one stride, scoops me into his arms, and carries me to my bedroom.

"Sacha!" I protest, but only verbally. I guess we are moving this to the bedroom, I guess I'm okay with a scenery change if he uses that talented tongue again.

"Bailey." He sets me down in front of him and grasps my shoulders. His face might be more serious than I've ever seen him before. "Beast, I am so sorry for this. I had no idea this would happen."

"What's going on?" I ask.

I hear the front door of the cabin open. Sacha slams the bedroom door closed, blocking us from anyone's vision, and preventing me from seeing who is walking

into the cabin. I finally take the time to pull my dress back over my breasts.

"I didn't know they were coming this weekend, I promise you," he says.

"Who is out there?" I ask.

"Hello!" A peppy female voice coos from the next room. "Sacha! Come out and say hello! You can't hide from us."

"Son?" A gruffer masculine voice calls.

"Is that?" My throat goes dry.

"Bay, it's my parents."

"Your parents?" I squeak, shrinking back from him. "What should I do? Hide?" I ask. The room is small. There's not even a closet or wardrobe to hide in. My suitcase takes up most of the empty floorspace.

"Hide?" His brows furrow.

"I could leave through the window? Find somewhere to stay in the woods until they are gone?" I suggest. "Or you could create a distraction?"

"Goodness woman, no," he reaches for my hands, physically stopping me from crawling under the bed, "what has you thinking you need to hide?" He pulls me close, tucking an arm around my waist.

"Because we aren't really—because the contract—I thought you didn't want people to know—" My words get very quiet. Being in his arms, the panic in my chest is starting to subside. I let myself lean against him a little harder.

"They already know." He speaks very low in my ear.

"What?" I whisper, the fear squeezing my stomach again. How could he tell people when I don't even know yet what I want him to tell? "You told them?"

"No, Bailey, they can scent it." He sighs. "Bigfoots have a much better sense of smell than humans."

"What *exactly* are they going to know?"

"They will already know I'm here with a woman, and the minute that you meet them, they'll know that we—were intimate."

My stomach turns. Fuck. "They can smell—that?"

"Yes," he says, "I'm sorry. I didn't know they would be here."

"It's okay, it's alright," I say, trying to convince myself more than I am trying to convince him. "So, I walk out there and meet your parents. That's not too hard."

I have never met a boyfriend's parents before. Not since high school at least. I don't usually let relationships get that serious. Breakups are easy compared to awkwardly meeting someone's whole family over Christmas. Spending holidays alone means I don't have to worry about buying anyone else presents.

"I know this is a big step for human relationships. I didn't expect to take it today."

"Okay, sure, right, of course," I repeat, but I don't think he believes me.

"I'm sorry, Bailey. They will love you."

"They are going to love that their rich son is fucking his assistant?" I mutter.

"They will love you." He wraps his thumb and forefinger around my chin, pulling back far enough to look me in the eye. "They can be really intense. If you want to stay in here for a while, collect your thoughts. Whatever you need. I am on your timeline."

Dammit. It's hard to be mad at him when he talks like that.

"Can I have a few minutes? By myself? Before I go out there?"

"Of course you can. As much as you need. I'll go out there and explain." His eyes soften, and he flashes that beautiful, confident grin that seems to pop up just to throw my balance off kilter. Things were going so well, so easily, I don't know if I'm ready to add his parents to this equation.

25

DISTINCTIVELY RED PALM

SACHA

Wrapping a blanket from the bed around my waist, I step into the main room of the cabin without Bailey. If she needs a chance to collect herself, I'll give it to her. I'll give her anything she wants.

I know it's too soon for this. I wanted more time for her to get used to me—used to my odd cryptid quirks—before she met my less-civilized parents. I have no regrets about sleeping with her, but I needed the next twenty-four hours alone, to find the courage to explain to her that we are meant to be together forever. Instead, I have my mom standing in the kitchen area with an armload of dirty moss, and random mushrooms that she foraged from the forest.

"Sacha!" When she spins around and spots me her face lights up. She tosses her items to the table so she can throw her arms around me in a tight hug. I wince at her outfit choice—a brown tank top that almost blends into her fur and nothing else. She's completely naked from the waist down. She's just an inch shorter than me, with paler fur from her more northern heritage.

"Mom." I lean into her embrace and familiar scent. It reminds me of every childhood memory: the late nights around the fire, fishing, hunting, foraging for

food with my parents, and the long hours I spent reading alone, learning everything I could about the human world hoping that one day I could join it.

My mom leans back with a giant smile, her eyes scanning up and down my figure like she expected me to grow another inch when I hit my 30s. "You look good! I didn't know you would be here! So happy we ran into you! You should have told us you were coming!"

"It was just a last minute trip. I thought you were in the forest for the summer."

"Your dad wanted to use the smoker." My mom waves her hand in the direction of her mate standing in the doorway.

"Caught an elk." My dad, looking pleased, offers this explanation before he even greets me. He's much taller than my mom, with darker fur. In one hand he carries a large chunk of dead animal, that leaks small amounts of viscera onto the porch floor. He also carries his distinctive, unpleasant odor, somewhere between roadkill and skunk; it's apparent even from across the cabin. He's only wearing a pair of ratty shorts, which were probably a color at some point but now look to be mostly mud.

"Your dad has been obsessed with that smoker since you bought it for his birthday," my mom begins. "Are you staying for dinner?"

"I was planning to leave tomorrow, but if you two want some time alone, I could get out of your hair earlier—" I offer.

Mom cuts me off, "Of course you should stay! We hardly ever get to see you anymore!"

"It will be nice to catch up." My dad grunts as he steps into the cabin.

"Abe, do not come into the house with that!" She sniffs, then flashes me a wide grin. "And who is staying here with you? A young woman? A human? You finally met your mate!"

"Mom, please. Humans don't have fated-mates."

"Nonsense. Your cousin Boris is with that nice little human man."

"Anthony." My dad ignores my mother's request and crosses the cabin to stand near us. "Boris's mate's name is Anthony. They just moved to Puget Sound. We should visit them."

"Maybe we can go after Solstice," Mom says.

"If you could not mention mates in front of her—she won't be comfortable with that word—"My mother only scowls as I try to explain, until her eyes focus on something past me and her face lights up with glee.

"Oh, here she is!" Mom cuts me off again, and pushes past me.

Glancing over my shoulder, Bailey has emerged from the bedroom in a fresh outfit. Blue jean shorts and a flirty floral top that is still totally appropriate to meet the parents in, not too much cleavage, and just enough leg to look absolutely delectable.

"Bailey." I breathe out her name.

My mom beams and, before I can stop her, scoops Bailey into a tight squeeze that briefly lifts Bailey's toes from the ground. "So great to meet you. I've always wanted a daughter! I can't believe my son was going to hide you from us."

"I wasn't hiding her, Mom."

"Look at her! Look at you! She's perfect! You are gorgeous, honey! What's your name?"

"Bay. Bailey, really, but you can just call me Bay, if you want." My mate's eyes dart wildly from me to my mother and back again. There's a small amount of water welling up in her eyes. I step in before she can truly panic.

"Bay, this is my mom, Yvette, and my dad, Abe." My heart is racing. It feels vital for everyone to get along.

My dad moves the bloody elk carcass to his empty hand and extends a distinctively red palm for Bay to shake.

I start to intervene, but Bay is already taking his grip and giving my father's hand a firm shake. Abe smiles at her enthusiastically, showing far too many sharp predator teeth. "Are you staying for dinner? Do you like elk?"

Bailey, to her credit, smiles and gives a nonchalant shrug. "I'm not sure I've ever had it before, sir."

"Sir. Ha! Did you hear that Yvette? I'm a sir now!" Dad pounds his chest with his empty fist. "A respectable male, just like my boy."

"Maybe we should get out of your hair?" I target the question at my parents, but keep my eyes firmly on Bailey. She glances at her hand and inconspicuously swipes at the smear of blood my father left on her palm. "I can call our ride back earlier."

"Nonsense! You came all the way out here to have a nice weekend. Don't let us get in the way! You two just do whatever you were going to do, like we aren't even here." My mom waves her hand through the air dismissively.

Bay's bright blue eyes meet mine as she gives me a small shrug. "We could stay, if you want? The helicopter will be here tomorrow, no matter what?"

I nod hesitantly. I don't want her to feel pressured to stay here with my parents, who do not hide their monster behaviors like I've grown accustomed to doing.

They never even attempted to integrate with humans, preferring to adopt only the parts of civilized society that suit their lifestyles. Things like hot water from a tap and fancy meat smokers were an easy sell. Other things, like modesty, and table manners are far less popular with most cryptids.

"Helicopter?" My dad shakes his head. "This boy used to spend afternoons chopping wood to keep warm, and now he's riding in helicopters. Can you believe it?!"

"We are so proud of him," Mom tells Bailey, before shooing her mate toward the door, "Abe, you are dripping on the floor. Sacha, take your father outside and convince him to wash up before he makes more of a mess."

"She's just trying to get you alone and pry for information about your relationship." Dad leans conspiratorially toward Bailey, who thankfully grins.

"Don't tell the girl that! Now I won't get anything useful out of her!" Mom scowls.

Dad leans over and presses a kiss to his mate's cheek, erasing her disgruntled expression before she pushes him playfully away. Bailey catches my gaze before bashfully turning her eyes to the ground.

"Really though, Sacha never tells us anything about his life, and I need to know everything about you. Where did you two meet? How long have you been together?"

"Mom, please," I interject, "Bailey isn't here to be interrogated—"

"It's new." Bailey cuts me off, stepping to my side and slipping her hand into mine.

My mom smiles slyly. "See? Don't worry Sacha, I'm not going to scare the woman off."

Dad barks out a laugh. "Yes, we'll limit the childhood stories to the least embarrassing ones."

"Actually, I can probably help with the smoker if you want." Bailey steps past me toward the door. "I worked in a barbecue restaurant in college, so I know a bit about them."

Abe flashes me another sharp-toothed grin. "I knew I liked her! Smart cookie. Come with me, Bay! You can help me load up the smoker."

He waves a hand for her to follow him, and with one short glance back to me, Bailey follows him outside.

I hurry to put on actual clothing before racing outside to stop my parents from scaring my skittish little doe. My father has his smoker set up in a clearing behind the cabin, far from the tree line. My mom fills poor Bailey's ears with embarrassing stories from my youth, while my father details the advantages of hickory versus oak for smoking.

I'm worried their enthusiasm will be too much for her, but my mate laughs while she listens, and when I step beside her she slips her hand into mine, granting me her beautiful smile. My parents fill her ears with all the cringe-inducing moments of my childhood: how I almost broke my arm jumping from the roof with home-made wings, the way I was obsessed with human society, and the entire year I spent refusing to eat any green food so that my mom had to burn every vegetable before she put it on my plate.

Bailey graces them with a toned-down version of trying to learn to fish like a Bigfoot and falling on her ass in the water, leaving out the inappropriate parts. My parents eat up every moment of the story.

"Thanks for putting up with them. Sorry for the imposition." I lean in close to talk to her while my parents bicker about how long the elk is going to take to cook. The answer is, of course, far too long for any reasonable dinner time.

"Please. This isn't an imposition." She presses her hip against me. "Your parents are really sweet."

"I know this isn't what you expected your weekend to be like."

"Not really, no," she grins.

"I wanted to spend the whole weekend convincing you to keep dating me," I whisper, so my bickering parents won't hear. "I didn't want your last memories of me to be about the time I accidentally sat on a wasp and cried when it stung me on the ass."

She laughs. "You *don't* want me thinking about your ass?"

"I was six." I scrunch my nose. She laughs again. "I wanted you to have more lurid thoughts of my ass. I was hoping I'd get the whole day to get a few very different nude experiences burned into your brain."

"You think that's all it would take to convince me to stay with you? A whole day of sex?"

"I think it would be a great start," I admit, wrapping an arm around her and tucking her into my side. "I think you liked those sections of the weekend a whole lot."

Bay smiles, watching my parents bicker. "Actually, the whole weekend has been pretty good. Your parents are..."

"Embarrassing?" I suggest. "Overbearing? Loud?"

"They are really wonderful. You know that, right? They love each other, and they love you."

"Yeah. I know." I watch the faint, sad smile on Bailey's face. "What's your family like?"

She shakes her head and goes quiet as my parents rejoin us. My mom triumphantly declares that she is going inside to actually cook us dinner since the elk won't be edible for another several hours.

"I can help." Bailey leaps to her feet, leaving a cold wake in her absence.

She likes them, my parents, and my home. My chest feels tight watching her here. Every moment longer with her makes me more hopeful that my mate and I can make this work, together.

26

RELEGATED TO THE FLOOR

BAILEY

Dinner promises to be delicious, if a bit of an experience. Yvette makes the entire meal from items she foraged from the forest. Moss, mushrooms, seeds, pine needles that she arranges into dishes, while instructing me which things to chop, mash, or combine. Finally, she declares that it is dinner time, piles several things onto a plate, and places it in front of me, which Sacha promptly removes from the table.

"Some of this isn't exactly edible to humans," he whispers into my ear, swapping my plate for one he fixed for me.

"Is your mom trying to poison me?" I tease in a whisper. "I thought she liked me?"

"You wouldn't die," he winks, "just be in gastrointestinal pain for the evening. She doesn't entirely understand the human digestive system." He hands me a knife and fork, just as his parents begin eating with their hands, scraping their fingers across their plates and directly into their mouths.

I glance at Sacha, he seems chagrined by their behavior. In a split-second decision I decide to set down the silverware and copy his parents' behavior.

159

Sacha watches me quietly for a long moment, before his hand finds my knee under the table and he gives it a firm squeeze.

"It's good," I tell Yvette.

"Would have been better if there was elk on the table," Abe grumbles.

"Then our lovely human wouldn't have been able to eat until midnight," Yvette scolds, but Abe grins and leans over to kiss her on the lips. Yvette breaks into a smile.

They may bicker, but they are still clearly madly in love. It's nice to see the family that Sacha grew up with. It's nothing like my own origin story, but I feel like I know him better after meeting his parents.

After dinner, Sacha begins arranging pillows and blankets on the couch.

"What are you doing?" Yvette asks.

"I'm sleeping on the couch," Sacha says.

"Nonsense!" his mom bellows. "You two have to share a bed."

"Mom, we don't—human parents usually don't want their children sharing a bed under the same roof." He glances in my direction and I realize his real reason is he thinks I would object.

"You are grown adults! You don't need to be uncomfortable just for humanities' sake." Yvette shakes her head.

"We live miles from civilization because we refuse to be civilized!" his dad agrees. "Get in there and sleep in your bed with your mate!"

Sacha cringes. "We aren't—"

"Sacha, come sleep with me." I reach for his hand, it's clear that his parents think this relationship is in a more serious and stable place than we actually are. I don't have the heart to disappoint them, and I wouldn't actually mind sharing that big empty bed.

Sacha meets my gaze, and something changes in his eyes. "If you're sure?"

I squeeze his hand and tug him into the bedroom with me. He drops my grip the moment we are alone. The lack of touch makes me a little sad. He leans against the closed door, leveling a long sigh.

"I'm so sorry," he whispers.

"What for?"

"I didn't know my parents would be here. I know that's a big step. I—" he takes a deep breath before continuing, "I don't want them to put more pressure on you, if you aren't ready for this."

"Your parents are great!" I almost laugh. "Certainly a surprise, but they've been really nice."

"Do you like them better than me?"

"Maybe?" I tease.

His whole face lights up with his easy smile. Shit, I don't mind sharing a bedroom with him at all.

"Turn around." I order. "I need to change into my pajamas."

He grumbles, but turns his back and begins tossing a pillow onto the ground and pulling the blanket from the end of the bed.

"What are you doing?" I ask once my head is through the neck-hole of my night shirt.

"Doing the gentlemanly thing and sleeping on the floor," He says, as though it's obvious.

"Don't be ridiculous. You've been inside me. We're adults. Just sleep in the bed with me."

"Are you sure you will be able to keep your hands off of me?" He smirks.

I roll my eyes. "You're right, I won't be able to stop myself from physically mauling you. You're better off safely on the floor!" I shove past him and climb under the covers.

"No, no, no. It's too late. You said I could be here." He leaps into the bed beside me.

I don't protest, but I do turn my back to him with a loud sigh.

The mattress beside me depresses as he stretches out, getting comfortable with the covers and pillows. He isn't even touching me, but I can tell exactly where he's laying. Without even looking at him, I feel like I could count the inches between our bodies. The closeness has my whole body awake and thinking of things I would rather be doing than sleeping.

Sacha's parents are just one wall away, and I know with that impressive Bigfoot hearing, they would know everything we were doing. I'm trapped, wide awake, staring at the wall.

"What did you all do to pass the time in the evenings when you were younger?" I ask, clutching my blankets a little tighter to my chest, determined not to roll over and touch him. "You didn't have a TV out here, did you?"

His hair rustles against his pillow as Sacha shakes his head. "We played games, we sat around the fire and did crafts. Sometimes Dad would read out loud to us. They don't appreciate large parts of human society, but they've always loved human literature."

"That's really cute." I picture him tiny and curled up under the blankets with his parents.

"I think a lot of those books were the reason I was so determined to join human society."

"You seem really close. How often do you talk to them now?"

He shifts behind me, so his voice is angled toward me. "We only see each other a few times a year, but I talk to them almost every week."

"I like that," I say. "I wish I had family that close."

"You don't talk to your parents?" Sacha asks.

He must sense I'm uncomfortable because one of his hands strokes along my arm.

"You don't have to tell me, if you don't want to." His voice is gentle and understanding, which only makes me want to talk more.

"My parents had me really young, probably too young. My dad was in and out of my life, and rehab, until I was around twelve. Then he disappeared pretty completely. I hear from him every now and then. He's been in prison the past six months, so phone calls have increased. My mom was the one who really raised me, mostly by herself. I could always tell she sort of resented me. Dad wrecked the picket fence life that she always dreamed of for herself. I think I reminded her of him." I pause to take a ragged breath, glad that I'm not looking at Sacha's face while I talk. He moves closer until his nose tickles the back of my hair.

"Take your time, Beast." His thumb traces a little pattern over my arm, and his odd nickname settles my stomach for some reason. I lean back into his warm body.

"This isn't a story that I tell a lot of people," I admit, "I got accepted to college, no scholarships, but I was so happy to go. It was great. I was having a wonderful time. I spent a lot of my breaks with friends, and when I went home for summer, my mom had found a man to live with. She was pregnant, they'd moved in together, they were freaking engaged. She hadn't told me about any of it.

Their new house didn't even have a bedroom for me. I spent that summer couch surfing with friends. My mom texted me a lot, said she wished we could spend more time together, but she never actually made time for me."

When my voice cracks I stop speaking. Sacha doesn't say anything, but his hand sneaks around my waist to give me a comforting squeeze.

"I found out about my baby sister, and my mom's wedding from social media posts. She didn't even invite me to the wedding. I'm not even sure her new husband actually knows who I am to her. All it took was me going to college, just an hour's drive away, and she started a new life as soon as I was out of hers."

Sacha presses a gentle kiss to my shoulder. "I'm sorry, Beast. You didn't deserve any of that."

I groan as my tears start to fall. "I've been on my own since then. We're basically no-contact now. I haven't seen her in a few years, I don't get invited to family events, and I only met my baby sister once. She had another child after that. I'm not even sure where she lives now. I still follow her on Instagram, but she doesn't post as much as she used to."

"Beast, that's terrible."

"But I think she's happy. I guess. I hope she's happy. Is that weird to say?"

"I hate what she did to you, but I understand why you still want the best for her. You're a kind and generous person."

"It's just, she's still my mom you know?"

"I know, my sweet Beast."

"I think that's why I like helping animals so much. Fostering kittens to make sure they are cared for, to make sure they find the right homes in this world." I'm having a hard time speaking above a whisper. "And sometimes it's hard to trust people. When they say they care about me." He sucks in a long breath that glances past my ear and scoots himself a little closer.

"I do care about you, my Beast. That isn't going away." He pulls me tighter into his arms, his hands circling my waist under the blanket. He stays there, holding me, until the tears stop falling. Safe and comfortable, I fall asleep in his arms while my pillow is still wet with tears.

27

SHATTER SOME WORLDS

I wake wrapped in him, surrounded by his warm arms, his broad chest, his easy breath, and his hard body. One particularly hard part of his body presses against my thigh. My leg trapped between his legs as he tugs me close in his sleep. When I try to gently pull, away he tugs me back in with a low, warning growl.

"Stay. A little longer." His voice is heavy with sleep. His hand sneaks across my body, his thumb dancing under my pajama top.

"What are you doing?" I whisper.

"I'm savoring the moment," he murmurs against my neck, putting his hot lips on the bare skin that he can reach. His gentle kisses have my newly awake muscles melting against him as his thumb reaches the underside of my breast. "You said you would give me the weekend, and it is still the weekend."

I don't know how to admit to him that maybe I was wrong. Maybe I want more than the weekend. I wasn't supposed to catch feelings like this. I wanted to come back from this trip satisfied that I didn't want him anymore, and sure that he wouldn't want me anymore either. I was ready to take his money, and we'd both walk away happy.

Now, here I am, wishing I could just stay a little longer. Maybe that's what love really is? Always just wanting to stay a little longer. My hand squeezes his arm.

"We should get going," I say. "Our ride will be here soon, won't it?"

"Hold on," he says as his talented fingers creep over my body. "I only have a few hours of you left. And I need to make the most of them."

I start to protest, but he catches my words with his kiss, and I melt into the bed, letting him take slow, lazy advantage of me. Forgetting all my worries as his mouth works its way down my body, joining his fingers in all my sensitive places until I am gasping and grinding against him. Coming apart on his lips, and tongue, and fingers. He spends so much time that we barely have enough time to clean off, get dressed, and pack our stuff before we leave.

Yvette and Abe give us both long hugs. They are warm and comforting—the kind of loving, overeager parental figures I wish I had in my life.

I wave goodbye as Sacha easily tosses my heavy luggage over his shoulder before we walk down to the field to meet the helicopter. Sacha holds my hand all the way back to the city before he loads me into a town car.

"Thank you for the almost perfect weekend." He pauses to take a deep breath. "I'll see you tomorrow? At work?"

The hopeful hesitation in his voice makes my heart ache.

"Yeah," I say simply.

His whole face lights up when he smiles, he presses a chaste kiss to my cheek before closing the car door. The spot his lips landed burns the whole trip home.

I drop my overstuffed luggage in the living room and stumble to the kitchen, followed by Rhapsody, who rubs against my legs as I grab a glass and fill it in the faucet.

"Bailey, I didn't think you'd be back 'til later tonight." Margot appears in the hallway, her eyes wide with surprise.

"We flew back in this morning. Sac—"

"Shh!" Margot cuts me off with a loud shushing noise and waves her hands wildly through the air.

"What is wrong with you?"

"I don't think you want my guest to hear you say his name," she hisses quietly.

I raise an eyebrow. "I didn't see anyone in the living room—Oh!" I take in Margot's disheveled hair, the obvious absence of any clothing under her loosely tied robe. "You have a guest!" I announce louder than I should.

A slim, green-haired figure appears in the doorway behind Margot.

"Tatiana!" I say, again much too loudly. I do not seem to be able to regulate my vocal pitch right now.

Tatiana is wearing one of Margot's t-shirts and a pair of oversized gym shorts. "Hi, Bay. Margot said you were going to be gone all weekend."

I look from my roommate to my coworker and back again. "I got back earlier than expected. Great to see you, though. Water?" I ask, holding out the cup that I poured for myself.

"I was promised Gatorade to replenish my electrolytes." She grins in Margot's direction, having the impressive self-esteem not to look sheepish before putting an arm around Margot's waist. "You had a nice trip, though? Hopefully? Who's the lucky guy?"

"Just some really lucky guy," I say too quickly.

Tatiana raises an eyebrow.

Margot reaches past me into the fridge, pulling out a sports drink to hand to Tatiana. "Here you go, doll." She unsuccessfully attempts to herd Tatiana from the kitchen.

"Hold on, I want to hear about some guy who is worth the Temp's whole weekend." She sidesteps Margot, keeping her eyes locked on me.

"It was fine. We had fun. Nothing much to report! We spent a couple nights in his cabin in the mountains, which sounds like it might turn into a horror movie where teens get murdered in the woods, but it didn't. We had a lovely weekend, and nobody got murdered. It was a little awkward, but genuinely it was a really nice time." I freeze with a smile.

"So glad! Let's go." Margot tugs Tatiana's arm, attempting to lead her out the door.

"Wait, what happened? Why was it awkward?" Tatiana resists the pull, cracking open her Gatorade and taking a long swig.

"His parents showed up." I admit.

"What? He invited his parents on a booty trip weekend?" Tatiana laughs. This information gets Margot's full attention and she stops trying to remove herself from the kitchen.

"He didn't invite them." I sigh. "We flew up to his family cabin—"

"Flew up? How rich is he?" Tatiana laughs.

"—so they didn't realize we would be there, and he didn't realize that they were coming."

"Awful." Tatiana shakes her head.

"Amazing!" Margot says.

"What?" Tatiana looks at Margot like she's insane.

"Bay is trying to end things with the guy! Now you have a great excuse to break up with him! Was it awkward? Were they awful?" Margot asks.

"No. They were really nice. I actually really liked them." I take a deep breath. "They seemed like they'd never met someone he was dating before. They were odd, but really sweet."

"So, you had a good time even though his parents showed up?" Margot asks.

"Did you guys even get a chance to bone? That's the important question." Tatiana leans forward. "Who cares about his parents? How was the cunnilingus?"

"Well... He went down on me like three times, and I came a whole bunch. We only got the chance to do 'it' once, but when I say that it was amazing—" I breathe out a sigh. "It was like...world-shattering."

"You hit the jackpot. Don't overthink it. I heard cryptid dick was good." Margot shakes her head. "I've never gotten a chance to find out."

"Excuse you, you can't talk that way in front of your current sexual conquest." Tatiana puts a hand against her chest in mock horror.

Margot rolls her eyes, before turning to me with a sad smile, she knows my family history. "Cheddar, it's okay if you like him, and it's nice if his parents like you."

"Don't over think it, Temp. You keep dating that life changing dick!" Tatiana grins wildly. "Simple as that."

"It's just that I've kind of explicitly told him that I don't want anything too serious, but now..." I trail off. "I just don't know."

"I knew you'd change your mind." Margot rolls her eyes. "It's really obvious how much you like him."

"What do I do now? If he still likes me—" I squirm. "How do I tell him that I was wrong?"

"Cheddar, you are an adult. You know what to do. Talk to him."

I groan. I hate being an adult. I pick up Rhapsody from the ground and scratch under her chin.

"Or don't say anything. Just show up at his apartment in lingerie. I did that to a woman once." Tatiana suggests.

Margot gives her a sly grin. "And that went well for you did it?"

"Well, she fucked me three times that day, before the wife I didn't know about came home." Tatiana laughs. "So if you count that as a win?"

"Alright, I think it's time to leave Bailey alone, let her decompress, we have other important things to be doing." Margot nudges Tatiana from the room with a firm smack on the ass.

Tatiana giggles as she steps into the hallway, calling behind her. "Okay, but I want to hear all the juicy details later, Temp!"

Great, now I have to figure out how to avoid telling Tatiana that the great guy I'm fucking is our boss. At least her lingerie story might come in useful.

28

NOT TONIGHT

SACHA

The weekend will probably haunt me forever. I had a chance to explain everything to Bailey; that we are mates, fated to be together forever. Instead I was a total chicken. I didn't tell her anything because I was scared of her reaction and now it's too late. I'm certain I'm about to lose her. She'll take the money that she's earned and all I'll be left with is my memories.

When Bailey still shows up to the office on Monday, hope flutters in my chest. She hasn't given up on me yet. She hasn't given up on us yet.

I need her so badly. Spending the weekend together only furthered my cravings for her. I'm haunted by the memories of her body, her touch, her smell.

I try to distract myself with work. Our most recent project may have been completed, but there are a million other things to do, fires to extinguish, clients to woo.

But distractions don't help. I'm hyper-aware of her every moment in the office. The way her hips sway as she walks through the hall. The way she brushes her hair behind her ear. The way she laughs when someone makes a joke. The careful way she leans across me when she

brings me lunch, letting her breast graze my arm. Her scent is a constant invasion in my space, making my dick stiff with a single whiff. She smells like the forest. She smells like home.

After everything that's happened between us I don't want my little beast to feel cornered. I've made my intentions clear. She knows where to find me. So I bide my time, I stalk her silently, like a proper predator. She's already caught, even if she doesn't know it yet. I just have to wait for her to come to me. Even if all I want to do is throw her across my desk and lick her pussy until she passes out. Tie her to my bed and make her come until she's begging me to stop, and I can sink my knot in and squeeze one more orgasm from her. The way I plan to ruin her.

Once she gives me explicit consent to do so.

And then on Friday. It happens. She wears the skirt.

At first I think it doesn't mean anything. When I walk past her desk I get a glimpse of purple pleather. She barely acknowledges my morning greeting, her face glued to her computer screen.

A couple hours later I walk into her alcove to ask a question and she spins her whole chair to face me. She slowly uncrosses her legs and recrosses them in the other direction. The movement pushes the purple fabric up her thigh, flashing another glorious few inches of skin, hinting at the pleasures hidden in the darkness between those legs.

"Can I help you with anything, Mr. Kwatch?" She adds a curious lilt in her voice.

"I need to see you in my office, Ms. Thorn." It isn't what I'd planned to say, but seeing her teasing body language, I almost feel like I've lost control of my functions. This woman is mine, if she thinks that she can tease me like this, then I am going to take her.

"Okay, sir, I'm just finishing up these reports and then I can—"

"Now. Ms. Thorn." I interrupt with a stern tone. I push the door to my office wide open and gesture for her to walk past me.

"Of course, sir." She gives me a wry smile, that tells me this temptress knows exactly what she's doing.

The way she saunters past, the mesmerizing sway of her hips is far more exaggerated than necessary.

Boy, do I have plans for her.

29

HE'S A BEAST

BAILEY

Sacha follows me into the office, his large presence a delicious promise. He closes the door with a loud click. In the heavy silence that follows he removes his suit jacket, placing it on a wooden hanger and hooking it neatly on the rack behind his door. His large fingers find the shirt button at his wrist. I watch enrapt as he methodically folds the fabric of his sleeve, pulling it up to reveal thick, hairy forearms.

I swallow so hard I'm sure he can hear it. "Did you need me for something, sir?"

"Sit," he commands, pointing to a chair in the middle of his office. A small shiver chases up my spine but I follow his orders.

Then he starts on his second sleeve. His fingers folding a neat crease in the starched fabric before he rolls it neatly above his elbow.

Fuck. I am a goner. I thought this male had a hold on me before, but now that we've had sex I think I would do anything he asked of me.

"Ms. Thorn. Do you remember what I said about that skirt?" He asks as he stalks around the room,

watching me as he closes the blinds that cover each of the tall windows overlooking the street.

"This skirt?" I ask coyly, my heart hammers in my chest. He noticed. I knew he would, but I'm still thrilled. It's been days since he even touched me. He watches me like a stalker every day at work but hasn't made a move. I spent a few lonely, frustrating nights trying to figure out the perfect thing to text him, but every message I composed didn't say enough, or explained too much. I don't want to actually deal with my feelings, I just want him to take me.

So, I decided to wear the skirt.

"Do you remember what I promised would happen if you wore it to work again? Wore it in front of me?" He pulls the final shade closed, sealing us off from the rest of the world.

Now it's only the two of us.

Just me and him.

Alone together.

"I remember, sir." I manage to say.

If anything could communicate the message that I can't seem to find the words or courage for, it would be the skirt.

Still, my chest squeezes when his steps bring him directly in front of my chair. He towers above me, his tall frame casting a long shadow, but my body heats up rather than cools down.

One of his large hands lowers to his belt which he deftly unbuckles and, with one powerful jerk, removes from his pant loops. He doubles the smooth leather in his grip, and jerks his hands apart in a delicious snap of leather.

I gasp.

He grins.

"I told you I would fuck you in it."

I shift in my seat, pressing my hungry thighs together, not exactly sure what he has planned, but thrilled at the prospect of finding out. He puts the edge of the belt under my chin, and tilts my head up. Taking my attention from the bulge already growing in his pants, and guiding my gaze to meet his big brown eyes.

"Give me your underwear," he demands.

"Wha—what?" I stammer out.

He leans down, so close that his breath brushes my cheek. "Your panties. Give them to me. I don't want anything in my way this time."

He steps back, arms folded against his wide chest, the buttons on his shirt strain under the tension.

I suck in a small breath, but scramble to obey. Shimmying my underwear down, standing to step out of them without removing my skirt.

He holds out his hand. "Hand them over."

I reach out to drop them into his open palm only to notice that my hand is shaking slightly.

"Good girl," he purrs, closing his fist around the fabric, "And they are already so wet for me."

"Practically ruined," I agree.

He holds his fist up to his nose, inhaling deeply. A motion that has my pulse pounding between my thighs, and then slips the underwear into his pocket.

He wraps his large hand around the back of my neck, cradling my head in his warm hand; he dips down to slant his mouth over mine in a perfect deep claiming kiss. His tongue sliding into my mouth, demanding more from me.

He hasn't been like this before, I haven't felt this dark intensity from him, this promise of how it will be when he truly lets go; when I am wholly at his mercy.

179

This is the male who chased me down, and in this moment my every sense is filled with him, his masculine smell, his dark taste, his warm touch, the sound of the low growl building in his chest. His hand tugs deep in my hair and pulls a moan from my throat.

He pulls back. "Shh, you don't want the whole office to hear you getting fucked by your boss do you?"

"No, sir," I say quietly.

He chuckles, and circles me slowly like I am prey. His hand grazes lightly along my waist as he picks a position, standing behind me. He dips his face down, to press his nose into the crook of my neck, inhaling me deeply.

"You are already wet and ready to get fucked aren't you?" he murmurs. "My eager beast."

I shiver beneath him, and nod.

His hand pull up my skirt, slowly, exposing more of me until his fingers can trace across the bare skin of my thighs and dip between my legs. He kisses my neck as his fingers slowly explore me, and when his roving thumb glances across my clit. I let out another moan of excitement.

"Are you sure you can be quiet for me, my beast?" he asks.

"Yes, sir," I whisper.

He growls, "Call me that again."

"Yes," I take a deep breath, "Sir."

He shudders behind me, his hand still moving between my legs, teasing across my sensitive skin. "Good girl," he says, "But let's not risk it. Open your mouth."

I hesitate for a moment but his hand stills, and I immediately drop my jaw open for him. His unoccupied hand appears around the side of my face and he slips the leather of his belt between my teeth. "Bite down, beast."

I clamp my teeth closed around the strap.

"That will keep you more quiet won't it?" He asks as his lips travel along the back of my neck.

I give a nod.

His wide palm presses me down, bending me over his desk. He leans over me, the weight of his chest pushing me further into the flat surface. The cool wood bites into my thighs.

"Grab onto the desk, beast," he says. "And don't move a fucking muscle." His voice is rough and hot in my ear.

I wrap my fingers around the front edge of the desk, desperate for something to hang onto. Sacha's weight leaves my back, and then his warm hands work up the sides of my legs, pulling my already askew skirt higher and higher, exposing more of my bare skin to the air conditioned office. The heat of his touch slicing across my naked thighs keeps me warm, preparing me for him.

"Beautiful," he murmurs. "Perfect. You are doing so well."

I crane my neck wanting to know what's coming next.

"Don't move, beast." Sacha's voice has a hint of warning in it. "I have been thinking of this perfect moment since the day we met and I am going to savor it. You are mine."

His foot knocks against the inside of my ankle, urging my legs wider until I feel air brush against my pussy, highlighting the wetness there.

"Every inch of you is perfection." His hands move down, dipping between my legs briefly, before sliding back up and around my ass, teasing around the part of me that truly crave his attention. "It's better than anything that I imagined it could be."

I make a small noise of frustration, but he just continues to caress me with measured and subtle

strokes. Each a little deeper between my thighs, each a little closer to my pussy.

He presses a warm kiss to my ass cheek and I bite back a yelp as his teeth scrape across me.

Then his thumb brushes right up against my clit, and two of his long fingers meet my lips, moving in long languid strokes while his other hand pushes against my back, keeping me firmly pressed down as he toys with me, twisting his fingers and taunting until I am a panting drooling mess. Trying to push back against him, to get just a little more pressure precisely where I need it.

He gives a soft noise of satisfaction, then his fingers dip fully inside me, fast and warm and thick, as his thumb circles my clit in slow strokes.

"Look at you, my little beast. Being so good for me. Letting me use this hole however I want." His voice surprises me by how close it is to my ear. "Be a good girl, come on my fingers and then—" his mouth gets so close to the back of my head that I can feel his breath in my hair, "—then I'm going to fuck you into this desk, until I finish inside you so deep that you are forced to think about me all day long as my cum drips out of you."

I bite firmly onto his belt, determined not to make a sound as the orgasm rolls through me, and my body clenches around his fingers.

"Fuck yes, that's my good needy little Beast." His beautiful voice growls.

His fingers slip out, and I'm not sure when his pants were removed, but the next thing I feel is the heat of his cock against my pussy just before he sinks into me.

30

WOULDN'T DEMEAN YOUR TALENT

SACHA

Fuck. I'm going to come.

I'm already going to come. I don't know how long I'll be able to hold back.

She feels so good. Too good. Perfect. Ideal. My mate. Even if I don't win her forever I will never forget this. This fucking perfect moment where I have her under my control, under my thrall, under my body. I get to have all of her, the delicious dimples that run across her soft thick thighs, the curves of her generous body, her slick tasty cunt.

I slide all the way into her, nestling my cock into her heat. She moans. Fuck. I'm not going to last long if she makes noises like that.

"Quiet," I mutter into her ear. "You don't want the whole office to hear what a little slut you are, do you?"

Her eyes stay squeezed shut but she shakes her head to the best of her ability. I chuckle a little and shove in deep, grinding my body against hers. The large knot at the base of my cock pressing against her tight lips. Not quite inside her, but longing to be.

I want to dive all the way into her, mate her, bury myself in her all the way to the base of my knot, but I

can't do that to her here in my office. For now I am happy with whatever part of her is available. The hot wet heat, her gentle gasps and muffled moans are so sweet to my ears, they drive me to thrust harder, faster. I need her. I need whatever part of her I am allowed to have. My perfect mate in her sexy body, tempting me with outfits, letting me take her, claim her in my office. My territory.

"Do you want everyone to know what a perfect. Little. Slut. You. Can. Be?" I punctuate each word with a thrust. Pulling out and slamming back into her, knot deep. She presses back against me, I grab her shoulder and her thigh, gripping her tight as I pound into her. I don't want to hurt her, but a small part of me is excited to see bruises from my fingers mark her body.

My movements get more hurried, more desperate, until pressing deep inside her, I grip her ass tight against me as I feel my balls tighten. I have to bite the side of my own arm to stop from roaring as I finish inside her. Spurting my cum deep into my mate, marking her so that anyone with a decent sense of smell will know. She is mine.

Maybe not forever, but for now, for as long as I can keep her.

I collapse against her, pressing her smaller frame flat against my desk. Unable to stop myself from kissing the back of her neck over and over, praising her quietly.

I would do anything for her, anything.

"My good, beautiful, Beast, you take my cock so well." I reach around her to extract the belt still held tightly between her teeth. It's scored with impressions from her teeth and wet marks from her drool, there's a delicious satisfaction in her leaving a mark on me like that.

"Sacha. That was amazing." Are the first words that fall from her mouth. She half turns her body under mine pressing her mouth to my lips in an awkward but consuming kiss. Communicating so much with just a simple act.

The doorknob of my office rattles surprising us both. She jerks beneath me, but can barely move, and I snicker.

"It's okay. It's locked, my Beast." I grumble into her ear, and press another kiss against her neck, wanting more of her even as my cock softens inside her.

A knock sounds loudly.

"Go away!" I yell over my shoulder.

"Sacha. What the hell is happening? You are late."

"Shit," Bailey says, firmly pushing me away. "It's Mr. Loch. I was supposed to remind you about the meeting."

"Meeting?" I ask.

"The Horizon—something," she whispers.

"We need your numbers for the Horizon presentation!" Ness rattles my door knob again. "Are you alright in there? Should I break the door down?"

I pull back from my mate, cleaning myself with a handful of tissues and straightening my clothes, trying to return my composure to it's pre-coitus presentation.

"You have to go!" Bay attempts to straighten her skirt, but there's nothing she can do to disguise her kiss-swollen lips or her sex-flushed face.

The sight of her makes my chest ache. I don't want to leave her, I'd rather walk across hot coals than through that door right now.

Ness knocks at the door again, and I feel myself scowling. "Shit, I'm sorry, my beast. This isn't what I wanted."

"It's what I expected." She grins, but this isn't good enough for her, she deserves more, she deserves everything from me. "You have to go. Please. Before he gets suspicious."

I glance again at the door and back to my mate. I'm not leaving for him, I'm leaving because she asked me to. "Will I see you tonight?"

She winces but shakes her head quickly, "I'm sorry, I have plans. Saturday, tomorrow when I bring Rhapsody to your place."

"Then we'll spend the day together?" I ask without thinking. Needing, with my whole body, to know when I will get more of her.

"If that's what you want." She runs her fingers through my beard, smoothing it down.

"It's the only thing that I want." I pull her in close and press a kiss to her soft lips. She melts into me for a brief moment before she pulls away.

"You need to go!" She shoos me toward the door, and gestures to the desk supplies that we've knocked askew. "I'll wait here a few more minutes, clean up this mess before I leave. No one will even notice we were in here together."

That twists my stomach. I want people to know, I want to shout it from the rooftops, but I can be patient, wait until she's ready for everything I have to offer. Grabbing my jacket from its hanger I slip from my office through the smallest crack in the door possible, closing it quickly behind me.

"What the hell is going on?" Ness demands.

"Nothing." I insist and begin walking to our meeting. He says nothing for a moment, watching as I roll down my shirt sleeves and slip into my jacket.

"I see." A slow smirk crosses his lips

"You didn't see anything," I growl.

He shrugs his wide shoulders, "As long as you aren't too distracted to do your job."

I'm starting to wonder if the job is actually the distraction, keeping me from what I really want.

31

NOT TONIGHT

BAILEY

I have to set down a bag of cat supplies to lift a fist and knock on Sacha's door. When he opens it I'm greeted by the beautiful sight of him in a tight t-shirt and gray sweatpants; it shows off his thick legs, and hugs the package he carries between them.

When did males find out that gray sweatpants are pussy Kryptonite?

"Hi, beautiful." He leans against his door frame, his gaze takes me in before his face drops to a small frown. "I didn't realize you were bringing so much stuff. I would have met you in the lobby to help with that." He reaches for one of my bags but I sidestep him.

"No worries," I say, but my stomach feels slightly queasy as I enter his personal space for the first time. Now I'll find out just how much my own home doesn't compare to his. The front door opens into a living room filled with dark natural surfaces, raw edged wood shelves, a large dark stone fireplace, plush rugs, an emerald green sofa, a wide wall of windows with high dark curtains, and behind his heavy looking dining room table is a full wall of plants.

"Wow. Your apartment is beautiful."

It's not what I'd normally expect from a billionaire, but the space really feels like Sacha. In one corner is a large cat tower which matches the decor so specifically that he must have had it custom built. I set Rhapsody's carrier down near it, and unzip the fabric opening on the top.

"Is that her?" Sacha asks, his voice is tight, I wouldn't have noticed it a few weeks ago, but now I know him well enough to hear the nerves in his tone.

"She's probably a little uneasy about being in a new space, she might hang out in there for a little while. We like to let the cats decide when they are ready to explore." I explain. "Rhapsody will come out when she feels safe."

"It's alright," he says, "I can wait until she's comfortable."

A little pink nose pokes over the top of the carrier and Sacha holds his finger out for her to sniff. The cat brushes her cheek up against his hand.

Sacha beams over at me, his big brown eyes full of joy. My heart squeezes in my chest.

"I think she remembers you." I smile. "She's all caught up on her shots, and has been spayed. You've already filled out all the paperwork. So you two are good to go."

"Thank you for bringing her over," Sacha says quietly. "Can I get you a drink? Coffee? Soda? I have vodka and pineapple juice."

He remembered my drink order, my heart squeezes again. "A little early for alcohol isn't it?"

"You're not leaving already?" His face is almost crestfallen.

"Well, first I'd like to see the rest of your condo, to make sure everything is cat appropriate." I pull the checklist that the adoption agency provided from my bag.

"Would you like a tour of the apartment?" He asks.

"The adoption agency would like me to take a tour." I click my pen officially. He grins.

"Living room & dining area." He gestures to the space around him, but my attention focuses on the way his t-shirt strains around his bicep. "Kitchen. Guest bathroom." He continues, leading the way down a hallway and gesturing to each space as we pass it. The condo is huge, every room is decorated in a similar fashion to the living room; it's homey, cool, and cozy. A cat would be happy to curl up in any of these rooms. Hell, I'd love to curl up in any of these rooms myself. "There will be a litter box in the guest bathroom, and one in the home office." He points to another door further down the hallway.

"Appropriate, it's where she will do her business." I check a box on my sheet and Sacha flashes me a grin.

"My bedroom." He reaches the end of the hallway and leans one long arm against the last doorframe with a smirk, waiting for me to reach him.

I glance past him, into the bedroom, more moody dark foresty colors, more plush inviting textures, a huge four poster bed. It's easy to picture us sprawled across it together.

"Hmm." I step into the room and check off the rest of the boxes on my checklist. There was no doubt in my mind his home would meet the adoption agency's standards, but there's something I need to know for my own edification and not for the sheet of paper. "Could I inquire how often you have guests over?"

"A couple times a month. Sometimes I entertain clients for Cryptech, it's easy to bring them here where I have control of the environment." He takes a step toward me, shoving his hands into his pockets.

"And how often do you have guests in this specific room?" I ask, staring hard at the paper. I don't want to be looking at him if he says something I don't want to hear. Everything I need to record has been checked off so I scribble a little black box into the corner of my paper. "Because I don't remember having a discussion with you, about the number of people who'd be visiting your bedroom, before we signed our contract. I thought maybe we should clear this up. Especially if there are going to be more encounters between us like the one at your desk yesterday—"

His hand covers mine, stopping both my nervous doodling and my rambling. When I look up his expression is quiet and serious. "Only you, my beast. There's only been you since the first moment you walked into my office."

I suck in a breath and squeak out, "Great! Perfect!"

"And what about you?" he asks. "How many guests have crossed your threshold?"

"I'm the one conducting the interview, Mr. Kwatch. I'll be asking the questions." I swivel on my toes and head back to his living room, swaying my hips more than is necessary. I wore my good jeans today, I know he's being provided with an excellent view.

A low growl stalks me down the hallway, and a second later a pair of large hands circle my waist, spinning me to face him. I clutch my clipboard tight to my chest between us.

"I need an answer, beast." He's grinning but his voice is a low grumble. He tugs me close, pushing our bodies together so quickly that it makes me gasp.

"Just you," I say. "I haven't had anyone anywhere close to my threshold for a while now."

"Good. Let's keep it that way." He dips in to press a commanding kiss against my lips. When he finally pulls back he plucks the clipboard from my fingers and places it on his coffee table.

"I think that's everything I needed to see." My voice feels oddly quiet. "Did you have anymore questions for me?"

"What do you want for breakfast?" Sacha asks, pulling me with him as he backs to the couch.

"What makes you think I'll be here for breakfast?" I tease.

"That can't all be cat supplies?" He gestures to the three large bags I lugged across town with me.

"Not entirely." I admit.

"You brought an overnight bag." It isn't a question as he sits backward onto his couch and tugs me into his lap. I happily allow him, resting my legs on top of him.

"I was thinking that, since I needed to be at my boyfriend's place—" I stumble and then power past hoping he didn't notice my slip up, "that I might stay the night?"

"The whole night?" He watches his own hand as he strokes it across my thighs.

"But, if you aren't comfortable with the idea, that's okay. It was just a thought that I had. I know you didn't ask me to stay or anything so I won't be offended if—"

"Beast." He interrupts my nervous words just as I was ramping into full ramble territory. "I'd love for my girlfriend to stay overnight, and I'd love to fuck her in every room of this house."

My breath catches in my throat. "Then you are alright with 'boyfriend'?"

"If you like it?" His hands trace across the top of my jeans, sneaking under my shirt to graze over the skin of my stomach.

"I like it very much."

"I like it too." He gives me a sexy lopsided grin.

A small part of me is freaking out. I like him. I like him too much, too soon. When he touches me like this, it seems more important to have him, than to have the money. Still I'm more comfortable knowing that when he inevitably gets tired of me, at least I'll have his money to go with these pleasant memories.

I bite my lip, shoving back my nerves before I use both hands to pull my shirt over my head in one quick movement. His eyes immediately fall to my breasts, drinking in my carefully chosen lacy bra; we sit in a quiet moment while I let him enjoy the sight of me.

"Well, I like this even better." He tugs me close. I squeal when his mouth closes over my breast, but it changes to more enthusiastic noises as his tongue finds my nipple through the thin fabric.

First, we wreck his couch, leaving the cushions squished and askew, then I let him fuck me against his high-rise windows, my bare ass pressed to the glass for anyone with binoculars to admire.

He carries me to his bedroom to spread me out on the large bed, we spend a few hours just cuddling before things start back up again and he comes all over my tits.

When I head to the bathroom to wash, my insatiable male meets me again in the shower, spreading my legs and eating my pussy under the spray of the best shower head I've ever had the pleasure of using.

He orders delivery for dinner, pasta, because he's a genius and a gentleman. We're barely finished eating when he flips me over on the table and demands that I scream his name while I come on his cock. Eventually we fall asleep wrapped in each other's arms, sated, exhausted, and ecstatic.

32

BEDROOM. RIGHT NOW

SACHA

It's a beautiful Sunday morning to wake up wrapped around my human. She's spent nearly every night with me since the day she dropped off Rhapsody. Sometimes she spends the night in her own bed at her own apartment, but I prefer her in mine. It's been three glorious weeks of her divine smell everywhere in my apartment, in my office, in my fur, and still I want more of her.

Running my hands across the soft flesh of her tempting body I enjoy the erotic sight of the impressions that my fingers make in her thighs. She's the perfect size for me to hold onto, to wrap my large hands around, to nuzzle into while my hard dick presses into her warm body.

Being with her is so easy, part of me wonders if I never need to tell her that we're mates. If we stay together regardless, then what's the harm in not telling her.

"Sacha." She moans a quiet protest at my movements, rolling over until I spot the small bruise that my teeth left against her collarbone the night before.

"Did I hurt you?" I ask, running a finger across her skin.

"Just the right amount." She reassures me with a kiss before closing her eyes again. My mate has every reason to be tired after the gauntlet I put her through last night.

I shift my legs and a small meow protests from the end of the bed.

"I didn't mean to disturb you either, Rhapsody." I sit up, offering a finger to the cat curled at our feet, she rewards me with a brush of her cheek, but doesn't move. I scratch under her chin until she lets out a little purr. "Let me get you some food, huh beautiful?"

"Yes please." Bailey half-asleep words come out muffled. "And coffee, I'll suck your balls out through your dick for a hot cup of coffee."

I huff out a laugh, but what my mate wants, she will get.

I press a kiss to her cheek, she groans again squeezing her eyes shut before I extract myself from the bed, trying not to disturb either of the beautiful creatures, but Rhapsody jumps to the floor and diligently follows me into the kitchen. I feed her before opening my fridge and pulling out breakfast for my beautiful human woman.

The frying pan sizzling on the stove and the smell of warm coffee permeating the air finally rouses my mate. She walks into the kitchen wearing one of my Henley shirts, the open neckline offering a beautiful tease of her unsupported breasts and wonderful glimpses of her thick thighs when she moves. A deep primal desire is satisfied seeing my mate in my clothing. She's mine.

"Something smells delicious." She grins.

"I'm making pancakes, bacon, and eggs." I gesture to the stove.

"I love that you can cook." She leans on the counter beside me, letting her hip bump against me before she presses a kiss into the part of my bicep at her face level. "Do you know how sexy it is?"

I bump her hip back, giving her a low warning growl. "If you don't want me to burn the pancakes then you'd better calm your tits down, Beast."

She gasps in mock horror. "Oh, no! Sir! I promise I can be good until after breakfast."

"Go sit down, over there, where you will be less of a distraction." I motion toward the stool at my kitchen island.

"Yes, sir!" Bay gives me a sarcastic salute, I swat at her plump bottom as she moves across the room and climbs into one of my barstools. She looks completely at home in my kitchen. This is where she belongs.

"Do you have any plans for next weekend?" I watch her face intently for a moment.

"Don't burn my pancakes." She points to the stove, but sneaks a slice of already cooked bacon from the plate. "I think I'm free, or I can be free, if a certain person wanted me to be free?"

"I wondered if you might want to go outside with me? Away from the office and our little sex den." I flip a pancake, we haven't been in public since our very first date, nothing has felt like going out for. "There was somewhere I'm supposed to be next Sunday, and maybe, you might want to come with me?"

"I could probably be convinced to go outside." She takes a deliciously crunchy bite from her slice of bacon. "Somewhere specific you had in mind?"

"Next week, is the Summer Solstice. The longest day of the year. My grandma Mimi hosts big get-togethers, where the Bigfoots come together and celebrate the solstice." I explain. "It's a bit like a barbecue. In the woods. There's music, and games, and lots and lots of food."

"Your grandma?" Bay asks slowly.

"She's not exactly my grandmother, more like a matriarch for the whole Bigfoot family."

"You want me to meet your whole family?" Bay's eyes get wide.

"My parents will be there, they already asked about seeing you again."

"So you want me to save face with your parents?" She almost seems to relax at the idea.

I take a deep breath, "My parents love you, but it's me that wants you there. I am inviting you, for myself."

"Oh, okay. The whole family, all at once. Alright. I think, I might need to double check my schedule—" Her words speed up as her mouth catches up with her nerves.

My stomach sinks a little. "It's okay, Beast. If you aren't ready then we can wait. Mimi hosts another party at Autumn Equinox, or Winter Solstice, or even next Summer."

"You'd want me there next year?" She swallows, I cannot read the expression on her face. I flip the final pancake onto a plate, slide it across the kitchen island to her.

"Yes. Bailey. I do."

"Right." Her eyes fall on the plate in front of her, but she slips a hand across the cool stone counter and takes my hand, squeezing it encouragingly. "Yeah, I'd love to meet more of your family."

My chest feels tight at her touch. I tug her hand up to my mouth and press a kiss against my mate's fingers.

"Thank you, my Beast."

33

COULD ANYONE HEAR US

BAILEY

Sacha inundates me daily with photos of Rhapsody, claiming that she is the cutest cat in the world. He's adorable with her, even leaving work at a reasonable hour to be sure she is fed and taken care of.

I'm sex sore nearly everyday because it's impossible to keep away from him at night. Sometimes we even fool around in his office, banging quietly and illicitly makes it even hotter. He is sweet and genuine and really talented with his tongue. When Sunday rolls around I'm almost not even nervous about meeting his whole family. Almost.

Sacha drives us in a large white SUV with leather interiors that probably cost more than the house I grew up in. It doesn't have any trouble climbing the steep mountain roads to the end of a dirt path. We still have a twenty minute hike into the deep forest to the location where the Bigfoots have their Solstice celebration.

My chest is full of buzzing nerves as we approach, I slip my hand into Sacha's and squeeze it for comfort. The party is in full swing when we walk up. The weather is perfect for this, Bigfoots are everywhere. It seems like every kind of outdoor sport is represented; frisbee, soccer, dodgeball, kickball, everything. All played by large, mostly naked, Bigfoots. Hair flies everywhere. Dicks and breast flop freely in the sun. It seems awkward to me, but none of the other guests seem to even care.

I almost feel overdressed in my yellow sundress and white sneakers. I'm not quite ready to show off my body the way these Bigfoots do.

"You look perfect." Sacha assures me when I ask if my outfit is appropriate. He wears a shirt and shorts in line with human ideals of modesty. I hope he isn't doing it on my account.

There's a row of tables, piled high with food. Every type of meat imaginable, some of it even cooked enough for human consumption.

Sacha's parents pounce on us as soon as we appear. It's really nice to see them again, they are just as welcoming as the first time I met them. Yvette immediately envelops me in an intense hug. Abe is pleased to tell me about the deer that he's smoked to perfection for the party, immediately launching into a story about finding the perfect white oak to chop down and cook with. It's charming.

Despite Sacha's assurances that my presence wouldn't be noticed, other guests seem immediately aware I'm a newcomer, and many take it upon themselves to perform their introductions. It turns out Bigfoots come in a bunch of different shapes, sizes, and colors. Some are a bit scarier or more pungent than others, but I'm surprised to discover the party isn't entirely Bigfoots.

"There are a lot more humans here than I expected." I say as we pick a shady spot to eat.

A few trees away sits a large human man, with muscles so well defined I can count the veins in his arms, his legs intertwined with the even larger legs of a Bigfoot. They laugh and feed each other fruit. Several humans intermix with the other groups of Bigfoots, along with sprinklings of other cryptid species.

"Plenty of Bigfoot have mated with humans. Particularly since the Decrypting." Sacha kicks a couple rocks out of the way before he spreads a large picnic blanket over the grass. "There's room for all kinds here."

"There are so many of you. Are all of you actually related?" I ask as we settle in.

"It's more of a community gathering. Mimi is the matriarch, she invites everyone, but we aren't all blood related." Sacha's hand creeps across the blanket to wrap around mine. "Before the Decrypting it was different. Bigfoots had to live in secret, so we weren't found out. These types of gatherings were the only times we knew where we could find one another. Now, since we can easily buy plane tickets and use cars, the events have started to expand."

We are nearly knocked to the side when a pair of child-sized Bigfoots chase each other across our picnic blanket and shoot off, dodging between their parents' feet, tackling each other with growls. A few adults carry infants close to their chests chatting as they watch the children play. The camaraderie of it all makes my chest ache. It's the kind of family bonds I've always longed for. I can feel tears pricking in my eyes, and I try to turn away from Sacha.

"Are you alright, Beast?" He asks.

"It's fine." I dab at the corners of my eyes. "It's just really nice to see everyone get along."

His arm slips around my side and he presses a light kiss to my cheek. "They already like you, you know. You'd be welcome if you wanted to come back, even if you didn't—want to come back with me."

My heart breaks at that thought. "Of course I want to come back with you."

"I will always be happy to bring you." His voice is a bit huskier than I expect as he presses another kiss to my cheek.

We spend the whole day with his family. Sacha even joins in on some of the games, although they look a little too rough for me, he seems pleased to remove his shirt and gain a few grass stains. As the evening gets later, the shadows get longer, and the crowd thins out, I find myself hoping, maybe, if I don't fuck everything up this time, I could join Sacha here again.

"I think we should pack up," Abe says to his mate, "Leave the evening to the young ones. We still have a couple hours walk back to the cabin for the night."

Yvette wraps me in another of her long comforting hugs, before the two of them disappear into the forest on foot. Their ability to navigate long distances is impressive, I have no idea which direction their cabin would even be from here.

"Can I show you one more thing, before we go?" Sacha asks.

"Alright." I say, not quite ready to end the evening anyway.

"The timing is just right, it's a bit up into the mountain." He gestures toward a path, "It'd be quicker if—if you don't mind—"

"What?" I ask suspiciously, folding my arms across my chest

"Could I carry you?"

I feel a deep blush rushing up my cheeks at how much I like that idea.

"You won't get tired?" I ask.

He shakes his head furtively and answers with a low growl, "I will not get tired, my Beast."

He picks me up by the waist, and with a shocking display of strength easily maneuvers me onto his back. My hands grasped around his shoulders, my legs wrapped around his waist. It's feels deliciously naughty as he starts to move through the woods, his back muscles flexing beneath my body. I assumed he was just looking for an excuse to be close to me, but he proves to move far faster than I ever could on my own.

It's impressive, feeling him run full tilt through the trees, totally in his element, dodging trunks and leaping over bushes. I squeak in fear a few times as he speeds up, but start to laugh as he eventually hits his stride. His broad hands supporting me to be sure I don't lose my grip.

"Here," he says, finally stopping to set me on the ground. We're at an overlook, high in the mountain, we've left all of his family and friends behind, several miles down the mountain.

And the view. The view is phenomenal.

"Wow," I whisper, leaning into him. I understand now, and his timing is perfect, the cloud cover is low over the mountains but there's a beautifully clear view of the valley below, misted in the colors of the sunset. "It's beautiful."

His hand circles my waist, tucking me against his body with a contented sigh.

"I always liked this spot," he says quietly. "I wanted to share it with you now, in case I didn't get another chance."

"This wasn't just a ploy to get me alone?" I tease.

"If I wanted you all to myself we never would have left my condo this morning," he grumbles in my ear. "I like when people see us together. I like that they know that you are mine."

The words bring a heat to my stomach. I shouldn't enjoy being claimed as much as I do, but there's something about this male that makes me giddy. I like the

feeling that I belong somewhere. I like that the place I belong is in his arms. Sacha's fingers drag along my waist, spreading the heat in my stomach everywhere, he has the ability to light up my whole body with one touch and a mild implication.

I turn in his arms and press my face into his chest. Soaking in his warmth, and his smell, and everything good about him, before I pull his face to mine for a kiss. He's soft, gentle, his big hand traces up my back, his fingers dig into the base of my neck.

I tug him a little closer, deepening the kiss, slipping my tongue into his mouth, trying to pull more from him. Egging him on by wrapping my teeth around his lower lip and fisting my hand into his shirt.

"Do you think anyone could hear us up here? Or are we completely alone?" I ask.

"Beast," he murmurs in a little warning.

"What?" I ask innocently.

"You know exactly what you are doing." He growls, but his hand brushes against the back of my neck, teasing the sensitive nerves there.

"I know what I want to be doing." I step away from him, feeling bolder, warmer, more sure of myself with each inch that I put between us. "I was just thinking about going for a run."

His eyes darken.

34

SCREAM SOME MORE

BAILEY

"If you are going to run. Then run." Sacha takes one step toward me. His feet crunching through the underbrush. "But I will catch you and a Bigfoot only does two things with his prey. Do you want to be eaten? Or fucked?"

My heart pounds in my chest. Fuck. I am already aroused.

"I can smell you now, little beast. I already know what I'll be choosing. First one," he grins, taking another step forward, "and then the other. Unless you are scared?"

"Fuck you, I'm not scared." My words are half a whisper, fear and arousal pump through my veins in equal measure, my white Keds slide across the moss underfoot.

"Then you'd better run, before I give you a reason to be scared." He grins, showing big sharp teeth. "You have until the count of ten, to get as far away from here as possible."

"Shit," I mutter, and then I turn and run. Behind me, I hear him dragging out the numbers, counting loudly as he watches me run away.

"One...Two...Three..."

My feet hit the dirt. I slip and scramble through the forest, no idea where I'm headed, a bumbling infant compared to the way that Sacha moved through the woods, but I can't stop the wild laugh that bubbles up my throat; a gentle burn aches in my lungs as a flush chases up my face.

I do not hear any more numbers, only my panting breath and the crack of twigs under my feet.

And then he catches me.

I scream as we tumble to the ground, and I try to squirm out of his grasp. My hands scrape against the ground looking for purchase, but large hands grip my waist, jerking me back and pinning me down.

"Do you want me to make you scream some more?" He chuckles, then his mouth is on mine and I lose all track of my senses.

His hips trap me as his hands jerk at my dress, exposing my breast to the summer air for the briefest moment before his mouth captures one of my nipples.

I card my hands deep in his hair, trying to pull him closer, pull him into me. His hands travel up my thighs to find my underwear before ripping them. Jerking the scraps of fabric away from my pussy, and then he's pushing his dick all the way into me, full and thick and hard. I'm already so wet that he slips in easily and I arch my back, pressing myself up into him as he covers me with his body.

But it still isn't enough.

"Knot me." I moan.

He rears back to look me in the eye.

"Knot me," I say again. He's silent but I repeat myself, answering his unspoken question. "Knot me, I mean it. I'm sure."

With a growl he pulls out of me. I start to protest until he flips me over, tugging my ass into the air. Pushing my chest down, into the dirt and sticks that cover the forest floor.

"Fuck, you are perfect." He shoves my dress up and pushes my thighs apart, "You are all mine, my mate, who is going to take all of me."

Humid evening air slaps against my ass, highlighting the wetness I know is smeared all over my thighs. I expect the press of his dick again but am surprised when his slick tongue slithers across my slit and traveling up to the pucker of my asshole. Rough noises leak from my lips to be trapped by the forest floor.

One of his hands covers my pussy, he easily slips in one finger, and then a second, stretching me to the point of fullness with his large fingers as his thumb works across my clit and his slippery tongue continues to press against my ass.

"Sacha. Sacha." The only word I can find in my throat is his name, as he works me until I am screaming nothing, coming on two of his fingers, and then he presses in three, and when he presses four into me I nearly lose the ability to speak. Melting into a puddle of loose muscles as his hand works me over and over until I am coming apart for him yet again, stretched and full and used.

Just as my body is sagging forward, his fingers leave me; my sensitive flesh still prominent in the air, on display for him. A large warm hand presses against my back, pushing my chest into the ground.

"My perfect beast, wet and loose and ready to be knotted."

I whimper in response, fear spikes through me, what if I can't take all of him, what if I'm not enough for him, what if I can't do it.

All those thoughts are lost as he drives into me with one strong push, settling deep into me with a grunt.

One hand digs into my hair and the other pulls my hips back to him as he drives into me again and again, pressing deep and grinding against me; there's not even a chance I could control his pace. He speeds up, thrusting faster, harder, rougher, his mouth full of animalistic grunts as he fucks me at a feral pace.

I lose myself twice, not even sure where my body is anymore, but he sinks all the way into me and holds still. I feel the thrilling thickness of him, his knot, the harsh bulge that meets my threshold with an insistent pressure he's never met me with before. It feels like it might split me open, tear me in half, ruin me forever, and I've never wanted anything more.

"Sacha." I manage to get his name through my lips in the haze of lust.

With one final growl he jerks me backward, I feel the tight stretch, and then the fulfilling pop as he slides his knot completely inside me.

I scream at the fullness, my body clenches and flutters around him, completely trapped and secure in his grip. My orgasm only seems to make him more wild. He grinds against me, driving me brutally into the ground, nothing coming from his lips but primal noises, before I feel him shudder and finish inside me. Hot spurts of his cum filling me.

"Fuck. Fuck. Bailey, don't move." His grip in my hair tightens and I make small approving noises as the pain swirls with the pleasure. "Fuck." He whispers again against my neck, his hips pump twice more and I feel him come a second time, emptying himself into me.

He twitches above me.

"My sweet little Beast. You make a true monster out of me." His hand strokes along my side and he presses a series of light kisses into my neck, already back to the perfect gentleman. The one who holds me and talks about how much he cares. He wraps an arm around me, tugging me close. "Are you comfortable? Cold?" He whispers and I nearly giggle.

He rolls us onto our sides, I feel the tug of his knot, still locked inside me, the way it traps us together.

"How long—until it shrinks again?" I wiggle against him to get more comfortable.

"Longer if you keep moving like that, Beast." He places a hand against my stomach, pulling me firmly against him. The heat of his chest warming my back. He growls in my ear. "Next time, we do this facing each other so I can see those perfect tits while I take you."

I sigh, pressing my face into his large arm. He's the one who is perfect, our time together has been perfect.

35

FOREVER FOR A BIGFOOT

BAILEY

By the time Sacha carries me back to the Solstice gathering, the clearing is almost entirely empty.

"Give me just a minute." Sacha sets me down beside a tree. My knees wobble slightly, he presses a small kiss to my cheek. "Wait here. I'll grab our things."

I giggle, leaning against the tree trunk for support, watching his butt sway as he walks away. My dress and knees are marked with grass stains, my white Keds might be 'formally' white, but everything feels light, airy, easy.

It almost feels like love when I look at him. Do I actually know what love feels like? The thought makes my stomach churn. My instincts scream for me to just take his money and run. His money, that's the sure thing, the rest of this is unpredictable. I'm safer if I leave behind the things I'm not sure of now.

Screw his feelings. Screw his heart.

Screw my own heart.

A large gray hand lands on my shoulder, startling me. I turn to see who it belongs to and bite back a yelp when I find the largest Bigfoot I have ever seen. She's stooping so much that her knuckles graze the ground and she's still a full head taller than me. Her long fur is

matted in some places, it's brindled gray and black and covers her entire body.

"Hello, Bailey." She smiles, showing large sharp teeth, but her green eyes sparkle and her voice is soft and easy. "I am glad our Sacha brought you."

"Hi. Sorry, I don't remember your name?" I ask, even though I am sure we haven't met yet. I'd remember speaking to a Bigfoot this large. She makes an impressive image, with her height and dark hair.

"I am Mimi." She lowers herself to the ground beside me, with the slow creakiness of an old woman. When she sits we are face-to-face.

"Oh! I've heard so much about you!" I feel myself relax a little. "Thanks so much for hosting this party! And letting me come of course."

"I am always happy to see a new face. I am glad Sacha has someone to bring, he was always special, he deserves a good mate."

"He is special," I say guiltily, watching as, across the field, he helps a Bigfoot family gather their two small children. "I hope he gets everything he deserves."

"He is going to. This is for you." Mimi speaks with a slow rhythm where each syllable feels carefully thought out. She presses a package into my hands, something wrapped in a linen bag and tied closed with a piece of twine.

"For me?"

"You are Sacha's mate aren't you?" Mimi asks.

"I'm not sure." I tell her. The word has come up before, but never from Sacha himself.

"It's pretty easy to tell."

"Is it?"

"We Bigfoot know instantly. Open it now, my dear." Mimi's soft green eyes twinkle as she gestures to the package.

I tug open the bag, pulling out a statue carved from white wood. It's small enough to hold in two hands, a stylized statue of a Bigfoot, holding someone else in its arms, a smaller figure, shaped like a softly curved woman.

Me.

It looks like me.

"It's beautiful," I whisper, tracing my fingers across the smooth wood.

"I'm glad you like it." Mimi leans back against a tree trunk, "I make one every time one of my family members finds their fated-mate."

"Fated-mate?" I ask. "What is that?"

"It's forever," Mimi says simply.

"Forever, as in…what, like marriage?"

"Bigfoots don't usually do marriage." She chuckles. "We don't need it, we just know, as soon as we meet each other."

"You think he knew if I was his fated-mate right away?" My eyes flick to Sacha, he's never mentioned this before.

"Of course he did." She grins. "We know, the second that we smell each other. It's fate."

"I'm not sure I believe in fate," I say without thinking.

"If you don't believe in fate then blame science. Hormones, pheromones, all the science stuff—" she lets out a low chuckle that ends in a grin full of terrifying teeth, "humans love their science. He already knows you are the one. He'll love you forever."

"Forever?" I catch Sacha's eye from across the field, he passes me a grin as he helps another Bigfoot wrangle a small child and two folding chairs into the back of a Prius. He's promised me so many things, surely he would have said something. If he knew. If we were meant to be forever.

"My dear Harry and I found each other almost a hundred years ago. I knew he was the one as soon as I sniffed him, but I still made him chase me." She sighs longingly at the memory. "He's been gone for almost twenty years. Never even saw the Decrypting. He would have hated it, was never a fan of human society. Probably would have liked you alright. He wouldn't have tried to eat you, more than once, I'm sure."

"That's very...sweet," I say, but my heart is still thudding loudly in my ears. "There hasn't been anyone since then?"

"There will never be anyone else. He was my mate. That's forever for a Bigfoot." She rests a hand on a tree branch above my head, using it for leverage as she stands. "You two have a good night, it's time for these old bones to get back into the woods."

I try to keep my smile pasted on, even though my stomach feels queasy. "Thank you for this, Mimi. I'll cherish it."

She nods, heading into the forest. I watch until she disappears, her figure easily fading into the woods.

I move from my resting spot and head for Sacha.

"Sorry for taking so long." He swoops me into his arms, pressing a kiss to my lips that I can't seem to rouse the energy to return. "Are you ready to go?"

"Yeah. I got to talk to Mimi for a moment."

"I saw, that's really great!"

"She gave me this." I hold up the carved figure. His eyes drop to my hands, his face changes subtly, but he doesn't say anything. I wait for several long breaths that feel like eternity before I start talking again. "Don't you think it's pretty?"

"It's beautiful, my Beast." He agrees, but lets go of my hand.

"It's us." I add quietly.

"That's lovely," He says as he climbs into his car.

I slip the figurine back into the linen bag and boost myself into his large car. Sacha glances at me but says nothing as he turns on the engine and pulls out onto the road. I chew on the inside of my lip, waiting for him to mention the meaning, to bring up the fated-mates, to explain.

Maybe he doesn't know what the figurine represents? Or maybe he just doesn't want to say I shouldn't have it? That I'm not his mate? My stomach twists at the thought of him leaving me for another woman.

I'm falling for him, like the idiot I am, wanting him to love me back, when he already knows if I'm the one, or just another stepping stone until he sniffs the right female. He already knows and he hasn't said anything, probably because I'm not it for him.

I don't have the energy or the bravery to ask him in the car. Not after our beautiful day together, and the way he made me feel so perfect and wanted in the forest. I should just leave now, take his money. Do it now, before I fall for him any harder.

"Is everything alright?" Sacha asks tentatively as we enter the city.

"I just—I need to stay at my place tonight. I'm tired and I'm out of clean underwear and–"

"No problem," Sacha assures me, but he can't hide the trepidation in his voice from me. "I'll see you tomorrow."

"Yea. Of course you will." I try to smile, but the turmoil in my stomach won't let me. I don't know if I can handle another person I care about walking away from me.

36

UNCONDITIONAL AFFECTION

I don't sleep well that night. I walk into the office twenty minutes late the next morning, with a wrinkled outfit and messy hair. I place the figurine Mimi carved for me beside my monitor. Even if it doesn't mean what Mimi thinks it means I like looking at it; I like the warm feelings it invokes of familial ties and belonging. Even if all of that is temporary I've decided to savor it.

And maybe to force Sacha to confront the truth.

I settle into my chair, opening my email and mindlessly clicking through the messages. My brain is so full of fuzz that I forgot I have a video chat scheduled this morning. I click on the link in the email distractedly, it opens a window to download some program for the chat.

"Bailey." Sacha's voice pulls my attention from the loading bar. He's standing in front of my desk in a pristine suit and a neatly combed beard, appearing perfect as always. He doesn't look like he was up all night worrying that I will never love him.

"Morning, sir." I smile, hoping I am reading too much into his clipped tone.

"You can't have that on your desk. Not where people will see it." He glances over his shoulder like we might have spies in the cubicles.

"What?"

"If someone recognizes it, they could figure out what—what we are to each other." He picks up the figurine, turns his back on me, heading for his office.

I leap from my seat, chasing after him, closing the door to his office behind us.

"So you know what it represents?" I ask, hoping he will give me the response I need to hear.

"The board members can't see this. If they realize what I've been doing. What I made you do—"

"You didn't make me do anything." I chew on my lip waiting for more.

He goes quiet looking only at the carving.

"Why didn't you tell me?" I swallow hard. "Why didn't you tell me that Bigfoots mate for life?"

"I didn't want to upset you." He exhales a long tired sigh, like he's been expecting this conversation.

"Why would I be upset?" I push back, and immediately regret it. "What's there to be upset about?"

"I'm a monster, Bailey, with set rules. The moment that we met, I knew what our destiny was. Humans don't operate like that. You needed more time." He takes a step toward me, I can't stop myself from retreating. "I wasn't sure if you would accept me."

"Am I just a placeholder?" My voice cracks at the question. I shouldn't ask, I know I'm not ready to hear his answer. "Until you find the right person?"

"No." He's beside me in two steps, towering over me, tugging my chin up so he can look into my eyes. "Bailey, it's you. It will always be you. It might seem extreme, but I've never met anyone who felt so right when we were together. You make me want more than just my job, or my company, or my money. You make me want a life. I want you to be my life, forever."

Forever.

The word clenches into nausea in my stomach and my breakfast threatens to splay itself all over his suit.

I pull my chin out of his grip, I can't have him looking at me like that, not right now. I like him, I want to believe him, but if he hid this from me then what else is he hiding?

"Fated-mates?" My mouth feels dry. "You and me. You're sure?"

"I've never been more sure of anything in my life, my Beast."

"Why didn't you tell me before? I deserved to know." I can feel that I am about to fuck this up. I'm going to yell, or cry, or lose my temper. Something that will show him I'm not worth loving. I'm going to ruin everything.

"I'm sorry. I should have explained," he says immediately, my heart skips a beat, "I should have told you right away. I should have trusted you. I shouldn't have hidden anything from you. I shouldn't have tried to bribe you into spending time with me, so that you would fall in love in return. I shouldn't have mated with you in the woods without telling you that I love you."

The floor seems to pitch below my feet, my heart feels tight, like it could break my chest apart. This big beautiful male is saying everything that anyone would want to hear, but I struggle to accept the offer of unconditional affection. People don't just love you unconditionally, not even the people who are supposed to, not even parents.

Love isn't reliable. My brain grapples for something that feels real, solid, dependable.

"The money?" I ask without meaning too.

"I'll stick to all of my promises, Bailey, say the word and the money is yours. Leave right now, and the money is yours." He's hovering over me now his hands clenching and unclenching at his sides. "But it won't matter what you do, you are mine forever. If you run, I'll chase. If you hide, I'll hunt. I'll always find you. I keep trying to change, to be more civilized, more human, but this is who I am, a monster."

"Not a monster, just a love-sick idiot." I squirm, looking at the door for escape.

Before I can move Sacha steps to me again and captures my mouth in his. A warm heavy kiss that feels like he's trying to prove something to me. My hands fist into his shirt, caught between fear and longing. How do you just accept an offer like this? How do you hold still and find happiness?

Someone knocks on his door and I finally push him away. He moves easily but there's pain in his eyes.

"Mr. Kwatch, we have a problem." Mr. Loch's Scottish lilt shouts through the door.

"Just wait!" Sacha yells to the door, not taking his eyes off of me.

"It's important Sacha." Loch is already turning the doorknob, and in a flash Sacha has put half of the room between us. My body is cold where he stood a moment before. Loch's gaze flicks repeatedly between the two of us.

"Is everything alright here?" Mr. Loch asks curtly.

"It's fine," Sacha grumbles.

"I'll just get out of your hair." I turn for the door.

"No." Sacha's voice is so sharp it could cut. "Bailey, do not leave until we've had a chance to finish our discussion."

I freeze in place.

"Ms. Thorn?" Loch's eyes lock on mine. "Are you alright?"

"I'm fine." It's hard to find anything else to say with the lake monster here.

"Then you are excused, Ms. Thorn." Loch waves his hand at me, but watches Sacha.

Sacha doesn't argue this time, so I gratefully flee the office. More than happy to get a few moments by myself to process everything Sacha said. To think about forever. With him.

I escape to the bathroom to clean off my smudged mascara where my watery eyes have ruined my makeup. I want to accept him, even though my instincts scream that it's time to run away from this commitment, the way I have run from every commitment. I'm starting to get tired of running. Wouldn't it be great to just stand still for a moment. Stand still and actually face my situation.

37

NOT TONIGHT

BAILEY

When I feel I've given Sacha and Loch enough time, I head back to my desk to find Chris from IT is sitting at my computer.

"What's going on?" I ask.

"Did you receive any strange emails this morning?" Chris asks, one eyebrow raised.

"No. Maybe. I'm not sure?" I say, my whole morning is a blur.

"Did you click any links? There's a virus on our system," Chris says. "Half of the network is down."

"Oh no," I mutter. "I downloaded a program for a video call..." My voice trails off as I realize what I did and I groan. "Where is Mr. Kwatch? Mr. Loch?"

"They left on very similar phone calls. Something about reassuring investors."

My stomach sinks. I've messed everything up, again. Sacha left without even saying a word to me.

This is the perfect time to run, there's no one to stop me, but the first place that comes to mind is running to Sacha. To find safety with him.

"Do you know where he went? What he's doing? I should be with him. I should help him."

"I was busy, Bailey, cleaning up the mess you made." Chris cuts back, his hands moving across the keyboard quickly.

"You clicked on the spam email?" Tatiana appears at my desk with a small laugh.

"I didn't know it was a virus!" I let out a groan.

"Don't worry about it," Jacob says. "Every time something like this happens there's a half dozen people who fall for the gimmick. Last time one of them was Tatiana."

"One time! I made the mistake once! It was ages ago!" She insists.

"It was six months before you got here," Jacob reassures me. "Everyone's done it at least once. I'm sure you weren't the only one who clicked it, we all got a similar email."

"I can't believe I did something so stupid," I groan.

"We all make mistakes, Temp." Tatiana grins, and then leans forward to ask. "Like how I left my jacket at your place, do you think I could come get it?" The question startles me out of my self pity spiral.

"Have you spoken with Margot since that weekend?"

Tatiana shrugs, but I see something wistful in her eyes, I make a mental note to bring it up with Margot later.

"Which weekend?" Jacob leans closer to ask.

"The weekend that the Temp spent with the guy she's banging." Tatiana deflects the attention to me with a smirk.

I glare at her betrayal.

"Oooooo, who is it?" Jacob's grin is wild, always ready for a bit of office gossip. "Someone we know?"

"Of course not! How could you have met? He's never even been in the office!" I squeak out, probably too quickly because Tatiana's brows nearly disappear into her hair.

Jacob grins wildly, "Come on, we're bored here. Give us something juicy."

I shake my head profusely.

"It's some rich guy that she is being super secretive about. She said he was a cryp–" Tatiana freezes mid-sentence. "Oh. My. God." Tatiana glances from me to Sacha's office door. "Is it...him?"

I continue shaking my head, scared to open my mouth.

She breaks into a wide smile. "You are totally hooking up with him."

"Who?" Jacob asks, his eyes are bright with excitement.

"We aren't! I'm not!"

"There's a reason Sacha has been in a better mood lately." Tatiana smirks.

"Really?" Jacob claps his hands excitedly.

Chris glances up from where he works on the computer, but doesn't say anything.

I try to laugh. "No, there isn't. I mean I did have a sexy weekend in a cabin in the woods, that part was true. It definitely wasn't with Sacha though. He's a big brilliant billionaire. He couldn't possibly want to be with a Temp worker who doesn't even know not to click on spam messages. I'm a mess! Can you imagine? What would he even see in me? Why would he ever go out with someone like me? Why would he want to be with me?"

The end of my ramble takes on a more serious tone as I word vomit my very real feelings. Tatiana must hear the edge in my voice because she pats my arm sympathetically.

"There's plenty of reasons he'd like you," she says quietly. "Jacob and I like you, and we have excellent taste."

Jacob exchanges a look with Tatiana, "Look, if you say you aren't fucking him then we believe you. We are furious that you haven't given us any of the glorious, juicy details, but you are a very easy person to like. He'd be a fool if he didn't want to be with you,"

"Thanks," I mutter, their reassurances do feel nice, but I have to talk to Sacha before I say anything to anyone else about the relationship.

I hope Sacha's alright. I think about calling or texting him, but I don't want to cause him more stress, so I twiddle my fingers and wait as IT moves in and out of every cubicle on the floor, it's going to take most of the day for them to clean up the server. One of the managers sweeps through our floor excusing people from work early.

Sacha still hasn't returned. All I can think about is comforting him. I want to wait for him. I want to see him again, hold his hands, and try to relieve some of his problems.

I enter his office, grabbing a sticky note and a pen to write a note.

Gone home. See you soon.

I pause and add.

Love you, Bailey

It feels right, it feels good. It's not nearly enough words to encompass all the feelings in my body, but it's as much as I think I can write on a three inch sticky note without crying right now. My urge to run away has completely dissipated. I need my Bigfoot. I only want to run to him.

"Ms. Thorn. I'm glad you're still here."

I glance up from the desk to find Magnes Loch's large green face peering through the door at me.

"Mr. Kwatch isn't here." I glance at the note in my hand and then shove it into my pocket.

"Actually, I'm here to see you, Ms. Thorn." Mr. Loch frowns, an expression I haven't seen often on him, the CEO seems to be the least guarded of the board members I've met, he's usually quick with a smile.

"Oh?" I swallow hard. I know I messed up with that spam email, and this feels like the moment. I'm going to be fired. Again. For my stupid behavior.

"Upstairs," Magnes says. "My office. Now. Please."

"Right." I know what happens next. This is the end of me at Cryptech.

Mr. Loch leads the way down the hall.

"I really think he's been a better, more rounded person the past couple months," Magnes says quietly as the elevator pings up upward.

"Who?" I shift on my feet.

"I haven't seen him this happy in years. I think you've had a positive effect on him and I hope he brings out the best in you too."

"I'm not sure I know what you mean?" I choose to play dumb. Does Mr. Loch know that I'm dating Sacha?

The elevator pings to a stop. The doors open.

"After you, please, Ms. Thorn." Mr. Loch gestures one large arm toward the door.

My heart thrums in my chest. How could he know? Sacha wouldn't tell him. This must be about the virus.

"This way," Mr. Loch leads us through a floor filled with cubicles, past his assistant's alcove and into his large office.

It's similar in layout to Sacha's with a wall of windows, and one of shelves, but Magnes's furniture is more modern, with a glass topped metal desk and sleek leather chairs. The room darkening curtains are drawn and a large fish tank is embedded in one wall, casting an eerie blue glow across the dim room. In the shadows of one corner is the telltale glow of Mr. Pleasant's red eyes.

"Take a seat, Bailey." The long necked plesiosaur cranes his head to look at the door, "the lights are dimmed so that Mr. Pleasant could join us for this meeting. If that's okay with you?"

I swallow hard. "Is something wrong, sirs?"

Mr. Loch sighs like he's in pain.

"Please, sit."

I wring my fingers in front of my skirt, and glance at the chair in front of his desk and then back to Magnes.

"It was an accident you know? I didn't mean for it to happen?"

"An accident?" Magnes asks.

"Obviously I wouldn't have clicked on the link if I'd realized. It was a busy morning, and the email said it was just a video meeting."

Pleasant makes a strange tittering noise in the corner. "She means the virus."

"Ms. Thorn. That isn't why you are here," Mr. Loch says.

"It isn't?" I ask.

"When we were clearing the virus from our network, one of our IT associates found a concerning item in your email," Mr. Loch says. "Do you know what we found?"

Now I sit down.

Chris. Chris, from IT, who I did not go on a date with, who doesn't like me, and I should have punched that night at the sushi restaurant. Chris overheard my conversation with Tatiana. Chris went through my files. Chris took it to HR.

"Ms. Thorn, can you describe your relationship with Mr. Kwatch?"

"I'd rather not," I squeak out.

"We know about the contract," Mr. Pleasant says, and it feels like my stomach drops from my body. "The one that you signed for Sacha."

The panic in my chest squeezes tight. Fuck. I am totally fucked.

38

BEDROOM. RIGHT NOW

SACHA

My day is long and stressful. Full of conversations with investors and board members, putting out fires, explaining too many times that these things happen, that no data was lost, that no one needs to worry. Talking until I am too tired to think any longer, and the words repeat themselves without any effort on my part. Hanging in the back of my mind the entire day is the sadness I saw in Bailey's eyes. I can't believe I hurt her. I was trying so hard to appeal to her human side when I should have just explained everything to her from the start. Trusted our bond. Trusted in fate.

I'm completely emotionally exhausted when I arrive at Ness's office late in the afternoon. All I want to do is find my mate, hold her in my arms and beg her to forgive me for being an idiot. I haven't spoken to her since this morning; I need to talk to her in person. To see her face, to hold her when I explain.

"What is this about, Ness? I have better places to be." I roll into Loch's office and plop into a chair, I'm slightly surprised to see Pleasant standing in the corner, I'd expect the chief technical officer to still be working with our IT team on solutions.

"Sacha. I'm glad you've been happier the past couple weeks. Don't you think you've been happier?" Ness slouches in his office chair. His legs are visible through the glass topped desk one of his legs fidgets nervously. He's not a sloucher, or a fidgeter, something is wrong.

"Could we cut to the chase? Just tell me why you asked me to meet you here?" I ask.

"We know about the contract, Sacha," Pleasant says bluntly.

"Contract?" I have a brief moment of confusion, and then my stomach sinks. This is about Bailey. They found it. "I can explain everything. I wanted to tell you, both of you. I was going to bring it up."

"I'm really disappointed, Sacha." Pleasant's voice remains calm but his antennae wave wildly as he speaks. "This is the kind of behavior I expect from Magnes."

"I would never. I don't pay for sex," Ness scoffs.

"The money wasn't for sex," I interject.

"And if I did, I wouldn't write down the agreement in legal jargon, sign it, and then send it through easily trackable company email." Ness's words bite through my protest.

"It's reckless, thoughtless, borderline illegal behavior Sacha," Pleasant continues. "Can you imagine if this had gotten to the press? You jeopardized the entire company. You could have ruined us all, everything we've built here. I can't believe you did something this irresponsible."

"I can believe it," Ness snaps. "He's been mooning over the woman since she showed up. Acting like she's his mate or—" he stops mid-sentence leaning forward to splay his large hands across his glass desk. "Holy shit dude, is that what this is?"

Pleasant's antennae sway toward me. "Of course she is."

"You knew?" Ness demands.

"You didn't? It was obvious that night at Moonshine, he couldn't stop staring at her."

"Why didn't you say anything?" Ness asks me.

I shake my head, "I needed to be sure that she wouldn't reject me."

"Well, fuck man," Ness mutters. His body language relaxes, he knows what it's like to feel this way, he almost didn't survive when his mate rejected him.

"We can't tolerate this kind of behavior from a CFO," Pleasant barrels through what is clearly a prepared speech, "we are suspending you from your position—"

"You can't do that—" I yelp.

"The board of directors already has." Pleasant manages to sound threatening without raising his voice. "We'll reconvene in four months to see if we can allow you back into your position."

"Pleasant. If she's his mate—maybe we should reconsider—" Ness starts to interrupt."

"We'll reconsider in four months." Of course the Mothman doesn't have any sympathy for my situation, the bastard's been strung along by the same human woman for years now. One who definitely isn't his mate.

"You can't be serious," I mutter. "This is my company the same as it's yours."

"Don't worry, we contained the information before it could present a real threat," Ness says, "We made sure Bailey was satisfied with the situation."

"What do you mean by that?" I sit forward in my chair.

"We fulfilled your contract with Ms. Thorn—" Pleasant says.

"What did you do?" I demand.

"We gave her the money that you promised her. We offered her another job with the company that was in no way connected to you, and she declined. She signed an NDA and took the money," Ness says.

"You gave her the money?" I stand, my hands reflexively ball into fists.

"We didn't have a choice. We're lucky she didn't try to take us to court. She wouldn't have ruined just you Sacha, she could have taken down the whole company." Pleasant's wings flutter with irritation.

"I don't care what it would have ruined! Where is she?"

"You should be thanking us, Sacha. You signed a sexual contract, the lawyers are furious. we saved your ass," Pleasant says.

"WHERE IS MY MATE!?" I yell, feeling the anger boiling to the surface. My fist hits the desk before I realize I've swung it. The room is quiet enough to hear the cracks splintering like lightning across the surface of Ness's desk, until the broken lines reach the edge, and the desktop shatters. Everything on Ness's desk crumbles to the floor in a rain of tempered glass. Pleasant flinches, but no one else moves for a long silent moment. My chest feels like it might burst.

"Gone. She's gone Sacha, she took the money and left." Ness scoots his chair calmly away from his ruined desk.

I don't listen to any more of his words. My feet take me to the hallway without any instructions from my brain. None of this matters if I've lost her. I have to find her, I have to explain, I have to make sure she knows that everything I said before was real. She is mine, forever and always, no matter the money, or the job, or some silly contract that never actually meant anything. None of that matters. I belong to her.

While I wait for the elevator I pull out my phone, calling her over and over, praying she will pick up. She isn't answering my text messages, and she's never listened to a voicemail in her life, so her mailbox is too full to accept new messages. I need to see her. I need to speak with her. To explain!

I growl in frustration.

The elevator is moving too slowly, I move to the stairs, taking them three at a time all six stories to the lobby. I don't have time to wait for a town car, or an Uber, or a cab. I need to see her now.

Fuck it. I am not a man, I am a beast, I don't need to wait.

So I run.

My bare feet pound the sidewalk, the wind buffeting my face. My suit feels tight, too tailored to allow for these movements, but I only run harder, feeling the seams split along my shoulders and back, hearing the ones around my hips tear.

A woman walking a poodle steps in front of me. I veer around her with a low snarl, not willing to stop, not willing to waste another moment away from my Bay, my mate. I cannot let those assholes at the office ruin everything for me.

I skid to a stop in front of her door, seams ripped and my chest burning for oxygen.

I pound on her apartment door.

"Bay! Open up!" I bellow at the hollow aluminum door.

"What's going on?" Bailey opens her door. My heart almost cracks in two when I see her perfect face.

Bailey looks me up and down before her face contorts into something that isn't quite surprise as she takes me in. "Sacha! You're here. Are you alright? What happened to your suit?"

"Bailey. I love you." That's all I can think to say.

39

—————

READY FOR A BIG COMMITMENT

SACHA

Her face changes, her expression softening until she throws her arms around me wrapping me in a hug so tight that I lose all concern she didn't miss me. She buries her face into my chest. It takes me a full breath to return the embrace, dipping my head down, pressing my nose into her, letting her smell fill me until a part of me breaks. I lift her from the ground, holding her against me, never wanting to let her go.

"I'm so glad you're here." Her words are muffled by my body.

"I love you," I repeat into her neck. Having her in my arms has helped calm my breathing, but my chest is still screaming for her.

"Yeah. I think you said that before." She chuckles gently.

"Bailey. I need you in my life. I love every inch of you, and every moment that we've spent together. I hope you can find it in your heart to forgive me for everything I've done, and please, please, take me back."

"Take you back?" She leans back, gently pulling away until I set her on her feet again. "Did you break up with me? I don't remember that part of our conversation."

"I was worried you would think—I didn't ask them to give you that money—" I run my hands up and down her arms, not willing to stop touching her.

"I didn't think you did."

"I don't want you to quit—"

"I know."

"I don't want you to go anywhere, I need you in my life—"

"I know. I know. It's okay." She almost laughs, reaching up to run her cool hand across my hot cheeks, smoothing out my beard. I catch one of her hands in mine and press a kiss to the meat of her palm. "It's okay. I didn't think you'd changed your mind about everything in four hours. I know you didn't tell them about the contract."

"I'm so sorry. I never should have made you sign that stupid document." I keep her hand squeezed tight in my grip. "I just needed you so badly. I wasn't thinking. It was such a ridiculous thing to ask you to do."

"It's okay," she soothes, "I like ridiculous things remember?"

My chest squeezes. "I thought you were running away from me," I admit.

She takes a very slow breath, "I think I'm ready to stop running."

I almost relax, almost, every muscle still feels full of adrenaline. "I don't know if I'll ever let you out of my sight again. I was so worried. I called you, texted, you didn't answer."

"I'm sorry, I didn't notice, I've been with—will you come inside? To talk?" She walks backward, tugging me with her into her apartment. There's a woman standing in the middle her living room. Not Margot. Someone tall and slender with brown hair tied up in a bun.

"This is Carlotta," Bailey says, "Carlotta, this is Sacha."

Carlotta's eyes go wide when she sees me. "Sacha Kwatch, owner of one of the largest tech companies in the world."

"Part owner…" I agree tentatively.

"Carlotta is helping me with a project," Bailey says. "I was going to have to tell her that my funding fell through, but then—well today happened and I thought I might as well make lemonade out of lemons. I'm sorry I didn't answer my phone, we were looking at real estate."

"Real estate?" I look between the women.

"Carlotta Miller, realtor," the woman holds out her hand for me to shake, "I've been helping Bailey look for space to rent."

"A space to rent?" I take the woman's hand without really thinking.

Bailey looks slightly embarrassed. "I called her when you first asked me to sign the contract. When I thought I was going to get the money quickly. We looked at a few places—"

"But, then she called me back about three weeks ago to say the deal was off, and then she called me again this morning to say the funding was available after all." Carlotta looks me up and down appraisingly. "I must say you've sent us on a bit of an emotional roller coaster, Mr. Kwatch."

"You are starting your cafe?" I ask Bailey, "For real?"

"Yes. I know it's a big commitment," she grins, "but I think I'm ready for a big commitment."

"I should get out of your hair for now," Carlotta says, gathering her things, "but I'll line up some of those showings for later in the week."

She leaves quickly, which is fortunate because I am already pulling Bailey back into my arms as the door closes.

"You can have your money back, Sacha, if you want it." Bailey lets herself be tugged toward me, but she doesn't look me in the eye. "If you didn't really want me to have it?"

"No," I say immediately. "No. It's yours, it belongs to you. I want you to have it, I want to see you succeed."

"Alright." She smiles but it seems sad. I just want to hold her until all her worries fade away, "I know I was never a very good assistant, and I was fired today, but there was one last message I was supposed to give you." She fists her fingers into my shirt and presses herself against me.

"It doesn't matter now, my Beast." I shake my head with a growl.

"It does, this one really does though." She swallows before reaching into her pocket and pulls out a sticky note she holds it out.

"It's okay, it doesn't matter anymore." I try to push her hand away.

"Just, read it. Please." She presses it into my palm.

I take the note, hesitant to take my eyes off my mate for even a moment but still, my stomach flips when I read the words written in her neat script handwriting.

"Really? You love me?" My hand tightens around her waist.

"Actually, I think Magnes left it for you." Her nose scrunches up.

"Then I have a message for him." I lean in and slant my mouth over hers, pulling us together until she's releasing a soft sigh into my mouth, eventually she pushes my chest away.

"Alright," she says as she steps past me, picking up her purse from beside the door.

"Where do you think you are you going?" I ask.

"To give Magnes your message." She flashes a smile as she fishes her keys out of her purse.

"Oh no you don't." I put one hand on the door, keeping it closed, and caging her to the wall between my arms.

She grins up at me. "I thought you liked it when I ran away?"

"You are a little beast," I murmur, "if you think you are going to get away from me that easily. I want to hear you say it."

"Say what?" She asks, her head cocked to one side.

I put a hand around her neck, not putting pressure, just pinning her to the wall, tilting her face up so she is forced to look at me. Her pulse jumps beneath my fingers.

"I want to hear you say out loud what you wrote on that note." My thumb traces up and down the column of her throat.

"I'm in love with you, Sacha." Her tongue darts across her lips, with a teasing smile. "I want to be with you. Forever. If that's still on the table."

"There will never be anyone but you, Bailey." It's an easy promise to make. I dip down to find her lips. Her hands reach for the side of my face tugging me to her. Not a passionate kiss, a compassionate one. Full of reassurance, warmth, and an unconditional understanding. She is mate, my perfect Bailey.

"Then maybe—we could try the knotting thing again?" Her voice is breathy when she asks.

"We can try it again, and again, and again." I tug her close, so she can feel where I am already hardening in my torn and ruined pants. Bailey's fingers toy with the lapels of my jacket in a way that feels completely erotic.

"Maybe you could finish ripping off that suit, chase me down the hallway, and ravish me until I am too tired to come anymore?"

"Is your roommate here?" I ask.

"She has her internship. All afternoon."

"Then we might need to hurry." I grin.

With the state that my suit is in, it doesn't take much to tear my clothing completely from my body. A few quick movements and I'm stripped bare. Bailey's eyes pause to drink me in, completely exposed to her from head to toe.

"Are you just going to stand there, Beast? Or are you going to give me something to chase?"

Her eyes light up, and she squeals before racing down her hallway.

I catch her before she can even get to her door. Wrapping my arms around her waist with a growl, I lift her over my shoulder and carry her into the bedroom. Her room is small and her bed is even smaller. I decide the floor is the best option for us, I spread her out under me. Her smile is bright as her hands rove across my body, digging fingers into my hair like she cannot keep from touching me. She's wearing a bright yellow shirt and a pair of blue jean shorts. I strip them off carefully, taking my time to tenderly kiss every bare inch of flesh that is revealed, enjoying running my fingers over all of her glorious curves and soft dimples, and relishing the way her breasts bounce as I remove her bra.

It's mine, she's finally all mine.

When we're finally both naked, I can smell the desire pouring off of her, so thick and delicious that I have to taste it. I lower myself between her thighs, to find her sweet cunt and bury myself in that pristine flavor of her. Seeking out her pleasure with my tongue, loving every second of the way she feels, the way that she reacts to me. The easy way her body concedes to mine as she comes apart on my mouth.

"Sacha, please. I need you." Her words are broken with lust. I love the way that she begs for me.

"The little office slut wants her boss to fuck her on the floor?" I ask, palming my own cock, it's hard and throbbing, but I need to stretch her first, to prepare her to take all of me. "Tell me what you want, Beast. Tell me how much you want my big thick cock in this sweet pussy and maybe I'll give it to you."

I slip a finger into her, and then two, she moans and grinds against my hand, her breast bobbing as she trusts herself down.

"Please. Sacha. I need your cock." Her face scrunches up tight with effort, "Your big thick knot."

"Where?" I ask, managing to slip a third finger inside her and she moans, her hand reach up, fisting tight into my shoulder hair for purchase as she moves against me.

"I need you inside me, in my pussy."

"Inside who's pussy?" I ask, pressing harder into her.

"Yours. Yours. Sacha. It's your pussy, to do whatever you want with."

"Good girl," I mutter, her cunt twitches and clenches around me, I cannot wait to feel that wrapped around my cock. "Fuck, Bailey." I pull my fingers out of her and she tugs my face down to hers, kissing me desperately, like she wants to keep kissing me forever, like it's all she's ever wanted.

The head of my cock naturally lines up with her entrance and we both gasp as I sink all the way into her. Pumping slowly, while she moans underneath me, her hips flexing up to fervently meet mine, until I cannot stop myself from pressing deeper. I wrap my hands around her ass, tilting her hips to change our angle and thrust deeper, harder, until the thick base of my knot sinks all the way into her. Her back arches and the noises in her throat stop for a moment as she shutters and flutters around me. Her pussy caressing and welcoming all of me. I empty myself into her, once, twice, and then roll us over so that she straddles me and she screams my name as she pulls a third release from my already exhausted cock before she collapses against my chest, and we are both panting, sweating messes.

"I love you, my Beast." I release the words easily, knowing there will be so many more chances to say it, and kiss the top of her head. "Was that as good for you as it was for me?"

"Yeah. That was a pretty great start," she agrees.

"A great start?" I laugh.

"A great start to forever," she says quietly.

I chuckle, stroking a hand up her naked back. Mine, she is my mate forever.

BIGFOOT BOSS

EPILOGUE

"I can do that for you." Sacha appears in the doorway leading from the storage room into the main room of the cafe. He moves to help steady the stepladder I'm standing on.

"I've got it!" I say, adjusting the menu sign behind our coffee bar. "Just stand back and tell me if it is straight!"

It turns out that four months is an excellent amount of time to obtain a business license, find a location, sign a lease, start sourcing local products, move in with your mate, and have plenty of time leftover for copious amounts of fucking.

Sacha takes a couple steps back, still scowling. "You don't need to climb the ladder. I am as tall as your ladder."

"Don't pretend you don't enjoy my ass being directly at your eye level. Is the sign even?" I demand.

He gives a small growl, before he answers. "The left needs to go up a little bit."

I adjust the sign and secure it with a screw before I climb down.

"Oh! it's perfect!" I exclaim, bouncing on my toes with excitement. Cat Rhapsody is opening tomorrow.

The pink and purple sign with the business name hangs above the counter, looking perfect in the freshly painted space. I can't believe my good fortune, to finally own my own small business, to use my hard earned degree, to have an amazing partner, to be standing on my own two feet without feeling like the ground might crumble beneath me at any moment.

Everything feels right at this moment. I might not know everything the future holds, but I have this. My business, my mate, my life, full of great things.

"You've done wonderful, Beast," Sacha whispers in my ear, he sneaks his arms around my waist and tugs me backward, his broad body supporting my back. "This will definitely be a successful opening tomorrow."

"Soft opening. Soft," I repeat. To test the menu and make sure the machines are in working order. I am trying to keep my expectations realistic, although it's hard to anticipate the worst when the past several months have been so perfect.

"It will go smoothly, and I will be with you every moment of the day." Sacha's help and advice has been completely invaluable over the past couple months.

"How are the kittens?" I ask. "You checked on them before you came here?"

"Yes. Aruba, Jamaica, Key Largo & Montego are all just fine. Settled in nicely. Rhapsody has relegated herself to our bed where they cannot bother her."

"Good!" I hesitate before asking the more important question, "And how did your meeting go at Cryptech?"

"Fine," he grumbles.

"Aren't you excited to go back to work?"

"Truthfully, I never want to be away from you ever again," he says with a sigh as his mouth finds the sensitive part of my neck that lights up my whole body.

"I never thought I could love being away from my job this much."

"But the board said you could come back?"

"The board agreed I could come back—" he stops himself mid-sentence. I pull away from him enough to study his face.

"That's great isn't it?" I ask. "That's what you wanted right?"

"I'm only going to be working part time for a while," he winces.

"Why the face? That sounds fantastic, Sacha. Really. You have always worked so hard. It's okay to take a break sometimes."

"Are you sure? It's less money—"

"Please, like I give a crap about your money."

"You only dated me for my money!" he declares.

"Yes, but I stayed with you because of your giant dick." I furrow my brows at his crotch. "That's still hanging around isn't it?"

"Would you like to check for yourself?" He reaches for me, but I pull away forcing him to keep talking. "Helping you open this cafe made me realize how much I miss the starting part of starting a business. I am proud of what we built at Cryptech, but I liked putting it together more than I ever liked running it once it got large. Not the way that I loved working with you, giving you advice, helping you build all of this from the ground up. I think there might be a way for me to help more people follow their dreams the way that you did."

"I think that's a great idea, Sacha. Your help was invaluable, you could do so much for the community." I press a little kiss to his cheek before moving toward the coffee counter. I bend over, stretching to collect the rest of my tools.

He makes an odd noise behind me.

"Are you looking at my big luscious ass again?" I tease.

"Can I ask you something?" Sacha's voice takes a serious edge, but I am having too much fun.

"How did I get such a big luscious ass?"

"No."

"Will I christen this new store by letting you fuck this big luscious ass on this counter?" I wiggle my butt and spreading my arms across the surface of the counter.

"No," he says. "I mean, I would like to revisit that question, but it isn't what I wanted to ask you." he wraps his large hands around my hips, lifts me, and spins me around so I am sitting on the counter. My stomach flips at the easy way he moves me. Heat already pooling in my stomach when his hands control me that way, but facing him is even better, getting to fall into his big brown eyes.

I dig my fingers into the fabric of his shirt, and spread my thighs to welcome him closer. He smells so good, he looks so good, he feels so good. I glance up at him through my lashes, already mentally planning which positions we are going to fuck in tonight.

"Then what on earth could you want to ask me?" I flutter my eyelashes suggestively.

Sacha reaches into his pocket and pulls out a little black box. He pops it open; there's a ring inside. A simple gold band and a large solitary stone, it's smokey brown with flecks of green swirling through. Moody, and foresty, and the most beautiful thing I've ever seen.

"Sacha. What the fuck is this?"

"A moss agate. Do you not like it?"

"I love it Sacha, it's gorgeous, but is this a—" My eyes flash up to his and the expression there stops all the words that were going to follow.

"Bay. Will you marry me?"

"Marriage? Aren't we already mated? Isn't that the same thing? Isn't that already a lifetime commitment? Do we really need a wedding? All the time and money and effort and—" I feel the word salad spewing forth.

Sacha catches my chin between his large fingers stopping my rambling.

"Beast. We are mated, forever, you are mine always. A wedding is a human custom that I thought you might want to participate in. So that we could invite all of our friends and family to come and celebrate our love. Now—" his voice comes out in a low growl that makes my breath catch in my throat, "—answer my question, will you marry me?"

"Yes. Yes. Of course I will." I reach for him. He wastes no time lowering his mouth to mine and dipping his tongue into me, and even if the cafe, or the city, or his business is just for now, he tastes like forever.

The End

ACKNOWLEDGEMENTS

Thanks so much for reading! A big fat thank you to the many people who helped me get this thing where it is today, with support, encouragement, and so very many comma adjustments: Meghan, Tara, and my own personal Carney.

I loved writing about Sacha and Bailey. Like many stories I've written this started as a joke when I mis-read 'crypto billionaires' as 'cryptid billionaires'. They will be seen again, there are currently two more books planed in this series following Mr. Pleasant, the Mothman, and Magnes Loch, our playboy lake monster with a heart of gold.

I love a monster romance and mostly write about big soft cinnamon-roll monsters falling into gross gushy love. I hope we can all find the perfect hairy beast to curl up next to at night, who will make us tea, read us a good book, and rip our enemies in half if we ask them to very nicely.

If you enjoyed Bigfoot Boss please consider leaving me a review! And then check out the other stuff I've written, and don't forget to stay in touch on social media!

ALSO BY LUNA CANTRIP

I Saw Krampus Kissing Ms. Claus

Being Ms. Claus kinda sucks. During my favorite holiday of the year the only thing anyone cares about is what my brother Santa is doing.

But when the famous Christmas Eve ride is threatened, it's up to me to fix it. And the only person who can help me solve the mystery is the little boy who used to pull my pigtails when I was a kid.

But Krampus isn't such a little boy any more.

He's all grown up into a seven-foot tall demon, with a penchant for punishment, and this year he has his sights set on more than just Santa's naughty list.

He wants me.

Will being thrown together light a yule log of romance? Or will meeting under the mistletoe be the distraction that destroys Christmas?

* * *

Winnie-the-Screwed: An MM College Romance

When Dracula takes a tutoring job to help ends meet, he doesn't expect Winnie, a hot bear shifter, to walk in and sweep him off his feet. He knows that he shouldn't act on his feelings with a pupil. But how can a vampire resist this honey pot?

Winnie needs to raise his GPA to stay off academic probation and keep his football scholarship. But he just can't stop thinking about his handsome vampire tutor, Dracula. Can Winnie contain his feelings until midterm? Will chemistry in the bedroom make him fail chemistry in the classroom?